SPACE CITADEL

They had landed on the forbidden planet of Boroq-Thaddoi.
They had made their way across the snow-covered desert
and the vast graveyard of mangled spaceships. Now they
stood gazing with awe at their destination, the Citadel.

The Citadel was unique in the galaxy. Some mad, brilliant
architect might have dreamed this blending of the arts and
materials of a hundred civilizations into a single monstrous
edifice, but no known race could have erected such a thing.
It dwarfed the nine walls of Skix, the great corridor on
Clotho, the ageless pyramids of Xhanchos, even the legendary cities of Old Earth in the proud and violent centuries
before the exodus. It was the monument of giants.

*Somewhere in the perilous labyrinth behind these towering
walls lay the secret that had eluded and destroyed all search-
ers for thousands of years . . . the secret that had to be
found before the Great Rebellion could begin . . .*

Also by John Morressy and available in Popular Library editions:

DISPLACED PERSONS

STARDRIFT

JOHN MORRESSY
UNDER A
CALCULATING
STAR

POPULAR LIBRARY • NEW YORK

6-29-78

Published by Popular Library, a unit of CBS
Publications, the Consumer Publishing Division
of CBS Inc., by arrangement with Doubleday & Company, Inc.

June, 1978

Copyright © 1975 by John Morressy

Library of Congress Catalog Card Number: 75-907

ISBN: 0-445-04240-0

For George and Jackie,
and all the Lawtons

PROLOGUE:

The Seraph

Three watches out from Dus'shk'kor, creeping at sub-light-speed toward a destination somewhere beyond the Belt of Avoidance, the driveship *Seraph* suddenly opened her atmosphere lock. For a time, the ship was host to a pair of small satellites. They tumbled through space at her side, gradually widening the gulf between themselves and the mother ship, slipping away to begin their own twin orbiting journey through the void. Then the *Seraph* disappeared into the invisible dimension of highdrive and headed at multiple light-speeds for the rim of the galaxy.

At the end of the next watch, Kian Jorry, master of the *Seraph,* summoned a ship's council. Settled comfortably in his solitary place at one side of the triangular mess table, he ran a hand through his close-cropped grizzled hair while his crew waited in silence for him to speak.

The crew of the *Seraph* were a varied lot, humans and humanoids in assorted sizes, shapes, and colors. All but one were present for the council.

Directly on Jorry's right, squatting on the table top to bring themselves to eye level with the others, were two Quiplids. Their names were Fimm and Jimm, and they were brothers. No one aboard the *Seraph* was positive which was Fimm and which was Jimm, and so the two were never distinguished from one another. It did not seem to matter very much to the Quiplids.

Next to them sat a big ruddy man with hair and beard so fair they were nearly white, although he was plainly young. His hair was long, and he wore it plaited in the style of the Skeggjatt battle-schools. He hunched his burly

7

frame forward, elbow on the table, a big hand supporting his chin, and glowered into the space before him. The Skeggjatt's name was Bral. Silent beside him sat Collen, the ship's defender. She was a Thorumbian, slim and pale-eyed, with smooth blue-black skin that gleamed like spilt oil.

On the third side of the table, farthest from Jorry, sat Dolul, an Onhla tribesman from the iceworld Hraggellon. He was a big expressionless man who seldom spoke. Next to him sat one who spoke not at all, a Thanist named Rull-Lamat. His head was covered by a hood, and the lower portion of his face was concealed.

Jorry cleared his throat and hitched his seat forward. The crew turned to him expectantly. He looked down at the table top in a solemn manner, then he rose to speak.

"My good friends and comrades, we have much to discuss. But as you know, I'm an old starfarer and a great respecter of the traditions of space, so I'd like to open this gathering with a moment of silence in memory of our departed shipmates." He folded his hands before him and bowed his head. Bral glanced at the others and then more closely at Jorry, but the captain's face betrayed no sign of irony. It was as sober as before. After a brief silence, however, Jorry looked up, grinned, and resumed his seat. "And now that we've paid our last respects to that pair of traitors, let's get down to business," he said briskly.

"Not meaning to question Captain's judgment, but are you positive they were traitors?" the Skeggjatt asked. "Saston never seemed . . . it's hard to think of him betraying us all."

"Vedniak didn't seem the type, either. He was a good fighting man," the Thorumbian added.

Kian Jorry smiled upon them paternally and said, "You're a trusting pair, and I like you for it. I was once the same way myself. But there's not a doubt in my mind about Saston and Vedniak. I believe my own eyes. I saw them taking a bribe from a Sternverein agent while we were on Dus'shk'kor. They meant to sell us out to the blackjackets."

8

"And that's not the worst of it!" one of the Quiplids cried, and the other added, "Tell them what happened in your cabin."

"I called them to my cabin during the third watch and put it to them directly, with Fimm and Jimm as witnesses. First they denied everything. Then they tried to bribe us into going along with them. In the end it came to weapons, and if it hadn't been for my little friends, I'd be out in the void and Saston and Vedniak would be taking you to your deaths in a blackjacket ambush."

One Quiplid said, "Traitors deserve what they get," and the other seconded him with, "That they do."

"So I trust that you're all satisfied, and we can proceed to new matters," Jorry said, looking around for negative reactions and seeing none.

"What about replacements, Captain?" Bral asked. "This leaves us short."

"It leaves us exactly right. Those two had no skill we need for the job ahead. We're well rid of them. We're ready now, Bral, trimmed down to good fighting strength. We have the crew, the weapons, and all the special equipment."

"We do?" asked the Quiplids simultaneously. "What's the job?"

"We do indeed," Jorry assured them all, ignoring for the moment the little men's second question. "Every planetfall, while the rest of you were off having a fine time, your conscientious captain was making purchases. And an occasional appropriation. I assure you, I took no time for pleasure until ship's business was completed."

"Jorry thinks of everything," said one of the Quiplids admiringly. "That he does," the other added.

Their captain nodded graciously. "I try my best. That's why the *Seraph* is a good ship. It has a first-rate captain, and now it has a first-rate crew."

"Not quite," the Skeggjatt muttered, and then was silent.

"If something bothers you, Bral, spit it out. I'm not like

old Captain York—peace to his bones. My crew can speak freely, and I listen. What's the trouble?"

The Skeggjatt hesitated before replying. His instinct was for battle, not dispute or discourse. On Bral's world, when men differed they fought, and whoever won was right. Jorry was a good-sized man, strong and quick, but Bral had no doubt that he could defeat his captain in open combat. And yet he allowed Jorry to do and say things that a Skeggjatt would not tolerate from any but closest kin.

The truth was, Jorry made him uneasy. He was too shrewd and resourceful. He seemed always to have the necessary weapon at his fingertips when the moment came. Even now, sitting across the table and smiling at him like a friend and brother, Jorry kept his hands low, out of sight.

And he was, after all, captain of the *Seraph*, and to be obeyed. Bral put aside all his half-formed thoughts of defiance. The habit of obedience was too strong.

"It's Axxal that bothers me, Captain. He doesn't belong in this crew," he said.

"Why not?"

"He's a Quespodon!"

The captain smiled patiently and said, "We all know that, Bral. Don't be so hard on him. Axxal's a good lad, with a good head on his shoulders. He'll be useful to us, I promise you."

Bral laughed. "What good is a Quespodon to anyone, Captain? They're all the same. One's as big a fool as the next."

"Axxal is strong, and he's loyal. To look at him, you'd scarcely think he's a Quespodon. He's not a complete fool, either. Accept my judgment, Bral. I say he'll be a help to us." Jorry looked around the table. "Does anyone else object to Axxal's presence?"

"Quespodons are stupid. Stupidity can be dangerous," Collen said.

"Axxal is not here to do our thinking. I do that. What about the rest of you?" Jorry asked.

10

Rull-Lamat made a gesture signifying contemptuous tolerance. Dolul expressed his complete indifference, but the Quiplids, as always, were effusive in their praise of the Quespodon.

"It appears that few of you want Axxal's company. You'll change your minds once we've made planetfall, I'm sure. Meanwhile, Axxal keeps to the machines and leaves us alone. Do the same. The issue is settled and we'll hear nothing more of it. And now, Bral, what else troubles you? I can read the discontent in your face, man. Out with it," Jorry said. His attitude was easygoing, but every member of the crew knew that his words were a command.

"Those birds, Captain. Noisy, stinking little creatures they are. I went near one of the cages and they nearly took my hand off."

"Must you be told to keep your hands out of a kiir bird's reach, Bral?" Jorry said.

"Why do we need those things on the *Seraph*? Where are we heading, anyway?" Bral asked.

"Ah, now, there's a sensible question, and I thank you for raising it. Our destination." Jorry nodded, as if satisfied to have come to this topic at last. "Well, you may or may not be aware of what I told our departed friends. They believed that we were on our way to Sternverein Headquarters to steal a payship. We are not."

"But why did you tell them that, Captain?"

"I had my doubts about their trustworthiness. It was a test, Bral." Jorry smiled genially at his crew. "They failed."

"Why not seize the payship anyway?" Collen asked.

"What loot!" said one Quiplid, and the other added, "And what a feat!"

"My friends, I'm surprised," Jorry said, looking solemnly from one to the next until he had met the eyes of each. As the silence lengthened and grew tense, he suddenly laughed aloud. "Did you really think that Kian Jorry would lead his friends into a blackjacket stronghold for a mere driveship full of cashcubes? I'd be taking you

11

to your certain deaths, and I know it. There are three full divisions of Sternverein Security troops on duty at that base—forewarned, now, and ready for us—and nothing will land on that planet or lift off alive unless they want it to."

The crew looked at one another sheepishly, and at length Bral, seeking to conciliate the captain, said, "We knew it would be hard, but we figured if anyone could take a Sternverein base, you could."

"Well, I thank you, Bral. I thank you all. It's true, I've done some fancy conniving in my time. Under different circumstances, I'm sure I could have brought it off. But I'd much prefer not to try plotting my way out of a black-jacket ambush. I have something better in mind." He leaned forward and posed the general question, "You've all heard of the Leddendorf ransom, haven't you?"

Most of them answered affirmatively, but Dolul responded with a flat "No" and Bral laughed loudly and dismissed the treasure as a legend.

Jorry smiled good-naturedly. When the momentary stir had died, he said, "It's no legend."

"No legend?" Bral retorted. "Captain, the tales I've heard of Leddendorf's wealth . . . how can a man like you believe any of it?"

"I won't deny that a lot of ridiculous stories have been spun around it—I've probably listened to every one of them—but that doesn't change the fact that the treasure exists. It's real, and it can be taken." At these words, the crew of the *Seraph* looked to their captain with new interest. Jorry allowed them a few moments to ponder the possibilities, then went on, "Since most of you are familiar with the story, I suppose you'd prefer I don't bore you by retelling it. . . ."

As he had anticipated, the Quiplids blurted, "Tell us, Jorry!" Dolul seconded them, and the others joined him.

"Since you insist," Jorry said, "I'll tell you all I know." He settled back comfortably, and began his account.

"Leddendorf was a merchant trader, sole heir to a commercial empire that extended over a tenth of the

12

galaxy. The man's wealth was literally beyond calculation. He had a wife and two children, but he seldom saw them. They lived on an isolated planet—regular paradise, I've been told—with a few thousand servants and attendants, and a small army to guard them."

Jorry paused, then leaned forward over the table. "Eventually, the inevitable happened. A band of pirates raided the planet, to carry off the wife and children and anything else they could lay hands on. It was a terrible battle. Only a handful of the defenders survived, and fewer than a quarter of the pirate force. The raiders sent back a captured guard—rather badly used—to tell Leddendorf their terms: His family would cost him half of everything he possessed. He paid, of course. Didn't hesitate for an instant. But he never saw his wife and children again."

Bral could not restrain himself. "What happened to them? Did the pirates kill them?"

"That's the general opinion. As you may imagine, there's been some colorful speculation on the subject." Jorry laughed softly to himself, and shook his head. "I once spent an evening on Barbary listening to a ragged old spacerat who claimed to be the oldest son of Lady Leddendorf and the pirate captain."

"Was he?"

"No more than you are, Bral. But I must finish my account. When it became clear to Leddendorf that he was not to see ransom or family again, he decided to use the considerable wealth he had left to buy the next best thing." Jorry scratched his neck slowly, frowned, and said, "Leddendorf spent the first part of his life amassing a fortune, and the rest of it squandering everything he had for revenge. Must be a moral in that somewhere . . . but I'll let it go for now. We poor struggling starfarers have other things on our minds."

"Go on, Jorry. What happened then?" one of the Quiplids urged.

"Leddendorf cultivated new friends. He invited his chief rivals to join him in forming a trading league with

13

their own private security force. That's how the Sternverein began. And if you've ever had a run-in with a Sternverein Security troop . . . they're a mean bunch." Jorry paused to run his fingers over the long scar across his chest. "A mean and brutal crew, indeed. But that's exactly what Leddendorf wanted: a force of troopers on every Sternverein ship, and every trooper knowing that if he brought back word of the family or the treasure, or captured one of the raiders who took them, he'd be wealthy for life."

"Did they catch the pirates?" Dolul asked.

"They never took one alive. Never, in all their searching," Jorry said. Then he added, "But I did."

"Do you know where the Leddendorf treasure is?" Collen cried, and the others put the same question almost at once.

"I'm fairly certain I do. We're on our way there now."

"Where, Captain? Where is it? How did you find out when no one else ever . . . ? How, Captain?" Bral demanded.

"You're getting very excited over a legend, my friend," Jorry said pleasantly.

"I believe it now. How do we get it?"

"We go to the citadel on Boroq-Thaddoi."

The reaction to Jorry's words was an abrupt, profound silence, as if he had spoken the unthinkable. Then came a babble of questions, most of them incoherent. Finally, Collen said simply, "That's a quarantined world."

"We've heard of horrors. . . ," one Quiplid said, and the other added, "Unspeakable things. . . ."

"So have I," Jorry said coolly. "I'm sure I've heard far worse than you. But with the help of my capable crew, I propose to land on Boroq-Thaddoi, seize the treasure, escape the horrors, and—to quote an ancient saying of my people—live happily ever after. Are you with me?"

"I've heard too many strange stories about that planet," Bral said cautiously.

"Have you heard of the treasure you'll find there? So vast it exceeds even *my* powers of exaggeration—which,

14

as you know, are considerable. There'll be single precious stones so big you can scarcely lift them. Every rare mineral in the galaxy, refined and minted and neatly stacked for loading. Armor and weapons and works of art by the old races . . . all waiting for us on Boroq-Thad-doi," Jorry said. "It's protected, of course. And well protected, too. We'd be fools to ignore the danger. But whatever can be hidden and protected can be found and taken. The question, my friends, is whether you're willing to run the risks."

"What risks, Jorry? Do you know?" Collen asked.

"Specifics are hard to come by. I've been putting pieces together since my first trip out," the captain said, grinning at his crew. "I'd have been there half a lifetime ago, but it was not until our landing on Dus'shk'kor that I finally got a positive fix on the planet. Q-worlds aren't on the charts."

"But what of the dangers?" Collen pressed.

"I've heard of traps, ferocious beasts, ingenious locks, bitter weather, age-old curses. . . . The last I discount, and the rest I've prepared for."

"How?" Collen asked.

"The kiir, for one thing. The fuel blocks, the climbing lines, the furs, the weapons . . . all those eccentric acquisitions I've made at every planetfall since we've been together, and long before, too. But the best preparations are right here, at this table."

"Where?"

"Right here, Collen. You, all of you." As he spoke, Jorry pointed to each of his crew in turn. "We have Dolul, a hunter and stalker from an iceworld people who have the gift of understanding beasts. And Bral, an experienced warrior. You yourself, Collen, are a qualified weapons master, without peer in twelve weapons. Axxal has the strength of any six men I've ever met."

"Are strength and battle skill enough?" Dolul asked.

"We have more. Rull-Lamat is a Thanist, an expert on alien ways. He can reconstruct the thinking of a vanished race and give us an idea of what to expect on their world.

15

Fimm and Jimm can climb a sheer wall as easily as you and I might climb a ladder, and I needn't remind anyone of the Quiplids' reputation for dealing with intricate machinery—locks, for example. I myself am an expert manual pilot. I can land the *Seraph* anywhere I choose to take her, without the aid of a landing ring. My other skills are known to you all."

Bral said, "We're a small band, Captain."

"We're big enough. There are no humans or humanoids lying in wait for us, I'm sure of that much. We may have to deal with some unusual and unpleasant forms of life, but we have the weaponry for that job. And since we don't have to face an army, why bring one of our own?"

"Just that many more hands to share the prize," one of the Quiplids said.

"Precisely. The only additional hand I had hoped to take on was a medico, but I found none I trusted. I have some small knowledge in that line myself, though, as does Axxal."

Bral laughed scornfully. "I'd sooner sew up my own wounds than have a Quespodon do me in with his clumsy stupidity."

"Enough, Bral," Jorry said in a soft voice. He went on. "If a man gets in harm's way we'll patch him up as best we can, then give him zaff leaves to keep him dreaming sweet dreams until planetfall. And then, if we're successful, I'll buy him a hospital all his own. Fair enough?"

"And if a woman falls?" Collen asked.

"Forgive my oversight, Collen. To be truthful, I simply didn't think of a weapons master as being vulnerable."

"We are," she said.

"Then you'll be well cared for. You're valuable to us, Collen."

"What if we're not successful, Captain?" Bral asked.

"Then there'll be no more planetfalls for us, and no need to worry about injuries," Jorry answered cheerfully. "I'll make no attempt to conceal that possibility. Boroq-Thaddoi is a Q-world. It isn't on any known star chart, and it's been generations since anyone landed there by

16

choice—except, perhaps, other seekers like ourselves. And they've not been heard from. It will be dangerous. We may all die, or lose our minds, or perhaps something worse—something we can't even imagine—will befall us. That's all possible. But I say it's just as possible—no, it's highly probable—that we can land on Boroq-Thaddoi, penetrate the citadel, and come out richer than all the planetary rulers in this galaxy."

Jorry paused to allow his words to sink in, then he said, "I hunted down a man whose father had seen the arrival of the *Drake III* on Pendleton, back in the twenty-five hundreds. It took time and some very generous persuasion, but I finally got the fellow to tell me what he remembered of the old man's story. It seems that every crewman aboard the *Drake III,* except for two, was dead. Some of them were still warm, others were long dead. The two left alive were raving mad. To this day, no one knows what happened to Commander Wright and First Officer Kooto, or how the ship lifted off and made its way back with a crew of corpses and shrieking lunatics, and the control room sealed shut with a skeleton at the helm. No one knows how those men were fed, and the sick tended, on a long journey. But when those poor creatures landed, all of the corpses carried green diamonds, and the smallest diamond of the lot was the size of my fist. The last survivor kept repeating, 'Boroq-Thaddoi . . . beneath the citadel,' until he died. Now, I don't propose to die raving mad, or disappear like Wright and Kooto, but I'd like the chance to be one of the richest men in the galaxy. We can beat that planet. Are you with me?"

The Quiplids bounced to their feet and stood erect on the table top, small fists raised. Dolul rose, and Bral and Collen, and at last the silent Thanist. Jorry beamed at his crew like a proud parent. He reached behind him and drew from a cabinet some small bottles of the mild beer-like drink of Dus'shk'kor, their last planetfall.

"My friends, let us have our last drink together as hard-working starfarers. It's meager stuff, but we're still

17

among the poor. There's a locker full of Stepmann green in my cabin; we'll save it to toast our success." He raised his bottle high. "To the wealth that awaits us on Boroq-Thaddoi!"

PART ONE:

To the Citadel

I.

The Plain of Convergence

Jorry was the first to set foot on the surface of Boroq-Thaddoi. He moved slowly, with unaccustomed clumsiness, hampered by his bulky garments. All the others, except for Dolul, were similarly attired and encumbered. The Hraggellon was no stranger to extreme cold; his body was adjusting rapidly; already his skin had lost its shipboard ruddiness and was growing paler, returning to the blue-white of Hraggellon days.

Jorry adjusted his eyeshield and took his first clear look at their surroundings. Under the cold and cheerless early light of its far faint sun, Boroq-Thaddoi was a forbidding prospect of black and brown, gray and dirty white. Its very appearance suggested a hostility to life that justified quarantine.

A wind roared across the face of the planet, unceasing, relentless, burnishing smooth the open tundra, abrading the boulders to roundness and honing the high crags to a knife edge. The contours of the horizon were sharp, but the ground beneath their feet was obscured by a snaking haze of blown sand and snow. The air was a cold and biting force that buffeted the body, sought out unprotected flesh, assaulted the ears with its whines and howls, and drew tears from unshielded eyes. Dolul alone stood it unmoved and unblinking. The sight of him caused the others to draw their thick furs closer around them.

Over their heads loomed the *Seraph*. She was positioned perfectly, erect on her landing jacks and ready to spring into space at a guiding touch on her controls. Jorry had had to bring her down manually; the early explorers

21

had built no landing rings on the worlds they quarantined. Landing was difficult on this uneven terrain—far more difficult than Jorry had anticipated, or would ever have admitted to the crew—but he had brought it off successfully. The first clash with the quarantined world had been resolved in his favor. It was an auspicious beginning, and Jorry felt more confident about future challenges. Nevertheless, he still sensed the tension of the landing, and when Bral saluted him with "Good piloting, Captain!" he responded irritably.

"Do you think I came all this way to wreck the *Seraph* on a Q-world?"

"No, Captain. We knew you could do it," Bral said, abashed. "We couldn't keep thinking. . . . A manual landing is always difficult, and on terrain like this . . . if anything went wrong. . . ."

"Did anything go wrong?"

"No, Captain. It was perfect."

"Let's get the gear in order and start moving before we're frozen to the spot. One final check before we move out," Jorry said, turning to the small mound of supplies and equipment.

They were setting out to cross the open surface of an inhospitable planet on foot, find and penetrate an alien citadel, and return bearing its treasure. They had only the vaguest directions to guide them, the scantiest knowledge of what lay ahead. Survival depended on preparation. The surface of Boroq-Thaddoi could be expected to provide nothing, so food and water for twenty watch-cycles was loaded on the low, broad sledge. Climbing and digging implements, fuel blocks for cooking and sentry-fires, shelters, and two covered cages of kiir birds were added to the stock, and when this was done, the rest of the crew stepped back while Axxal, the eighth member of their little band, tied the contents down securely and adjusted the harness to fit across his broad chest.

Axxal was captain's orderly and general factotum of the *Seraph*. Like all Quespodons, he was hairless, his body was broad and compact, and he was enormously strong; but he did not bear the mottled skin that marked most of his race. Axxal did his share, and more than his share, of the ship's work, and he did it well. He was loyal to Jorry, who always treated him with a degree of consideration seldom shown Quespodons by the other starfaring races. Fimm and Jimm admired him. The rest tolerated him. Even Bral, who scorned Axxal's race, respected his strength.

While Axxal prepared the sledge, Jorry distributed weapons. Each crewman was already armed with the customary personal weapons of his people, but Jorry supplemented these. On such an expedition as this, he wanted his crew outfitted with the best arms available in the galaxy. Axxal and Dolul were each given a pair of pistols. While they strapped them on and filled their pockets with shells, Jorry broke open a long crate and lifted out three short-range projectile rifles.

These were the most powerful weapons in space. Most of the warrior races mistrusted the crude firearms of the period and preferred to rely on blades. Their doubt was well-founded. The ordinary firearms of the twenty-seventh century were crudely made, and jammed or misfired at crucial moments; a man was foolish to trust his life to them. But these weapons, made by the artisans of Rugatcz V from authentic Old Earth models, were as close to flawless as the work of humans could be. Jorry trusted in them. One rifle he slung over his own shoulder, the second he gave to Bral, the third to Collen. Bral hefted his rifle and looked dubiously at the captain.

"Take it, Bral, and use it. I know you'd prefer your ax, but a rifle has a longer range," Jorry said. "You've used one before, I know."

The Skeggjatt spoke as if he were making a shameful mission. "Yes, many times. But I can handle anything we may meet on this planet with my ax. You've seen me use it."

"It's not a question of fighting skill, Bral, I just don't want anything getting that close. These rifles will drop an attacker fifty meters off. That's a comfortable margin."

"What if they don't?"

"Then you'll have a chance to use your ax." Jorry turned to Collen. "Can you handle everything? You'll be our chief defense."

The Thorumbian nodded. Even without the rifle, she was the best-armed of the party. Bandoliers of the deadly little finger knives favored by the Lixians were crossed over her shoulders, a pistol and shortsword hung at her belt, and at her back were a Toxxan longbow and a quiver of broad arrows. The rifle she held poised at the ready.

Jorry personally inspected each member of the party. When he was satisfied, he drew them into a tight circle in the lee of the high-piled sledge and said, "We move in single file until we reach the citadel. I'm first, Collen right behind me, then Fimm and Jimm, then Axxal with the sledge. Dolul behind the sledge, guiding it and spelling Axxal. Rull-Lamat next, Bral last. Whatever happens, don't spread out. Stay in sight of one another."

"Traps out there?" Collen asked.

"A lot of things out there. If we see anything moving up ahead, you and I open fire. If anything comes in from behind, Bral takes it. So everyone has to stay in place, and keep as close to my track as they can. If the weather turns suddenly—and it will, often—stand fast and wait it out. We can't afford to lose anyone, but we can't risk the group for one straggler, either. Remember that."

"Why not tie ourselves together on a long line?" Bral suggested.

"No. If anything got one of us, it would get us all."

"So it's everyone for himself," Dolul said.

"It's everyone for the group, until we're spaceborne again. Our chances of reaching the citadel are better if we keep close together on a narrow trail. We have to be on the mountains by nightfall. The nights here are long and cold, and we'll find a sheltered place to camp in the mountains. Tomorrow at nightfall, we'll be at the citadel," Jorry said.

"Why did we land so far away?" Collen asked.

"A precaution. Any more questions?" No question came, and Jorry said, "Then move out," and turned toward the distant mountains.

The *Seraph* stood near the central point of an upland plain that lay between two mountain ranges. One of the ranges was much higher than the other, and it was toward the higher range that Jorry led his small band.

Their progress was slow. Jorry picked his way over the uneven surface hidden beneath the low veil of driven snow and sand as if he were groping in the dark for a half-remembered path. All were wary. The footing was uncertain on this rough, rock-strewn ground, and often the dim light was blocked by a sudden mass of heavy clouds that rolled overhead. In their wake came brief blinding assaults of snow.

The party came halfway to the mountains without incident. The ground had risen slowly, and unexpectedly they found themselves on a ridge overlooking a slope that led to a wide saucer-shaped depression dotted with boulders. Jorry proposed a rest when they reached the other side.

Boulders higher than the tallest among them were scattered over the floor of the depression. All appeared to be resting lightly on the surface, unlike the deep-buried rocks of the upper plains. Jorry commented on this to Collen.

"They're not meteors," Collen said.

"No, meteors would be buried. These look as if they were put down gently."

"They're not volcanic, either. There are no volcanoes. Maybe the wind. . . ," Collen began. Jorry gave her a curious glance and the Thorumbian explained, "The wind might have blown away all the surrounding sand, over the course of time. That's possible."

"Maybe so," Jorry said. But he wondered still.

Snow-squalls forced them to halt twice, but the crossing was otherwise uneventful until they reached the center. The low rim of the depression encircled them, equidistant in all directions. The upper portions of the mountain range loomed ahead. Suddenly a low rumble

25

arose all around them. It grew in volume rapidly. The riflemen leveled their weapons for an attack, but no one and nothing could be seen. The sound grew ever louder, and then the ground began to move beneath their feet.

"It's sinking! We're going down!" Axxal cried.

Jorry spread his feet more widely, looked about, and saw the boulders moving. "Run! To the rim, as fast as you can! Axxal, Bral, help with the sledge!" he cried, and started forward in the lead.

All around them, the boulders that rested so lightly on the surface were trembling and shifting. Some were already beginning to roll toward their little caravan as the center of the depression sank ever lower. Their only hope was to reach the rim before all the boulders rolled inward and downward to converge on them as they struggled against the ever-steepening upward path.

It was Axxal who saved them. Leaving the sledge to Dolul and Bral, he took upon himself the task of warding off the rocks that were coming at them with increasing speed and frequency. The first few were moving slowly, and could be turned aside by a single strong thrust; but as their speed increased, Axxal's work became perilous. He stopped one stone nearly his own size, and lifting it high, hurled it with all his strength at a boulder heading directly for the sledge. The boulder was diverted. Twice he repeated this feat, and then they were past the danger point. They had reached the rim, and the stones that had been scattered at random over the floor of the shallow crater now lay in a compacted heap behind them, at the sunken center of the crater.

On high level ground beyond the rim they slumped and sprawled and rested from their frantic exertions. Axxal's leathery palms were scraped and raw, and the mark of the harness was scored deep into Dolul's bare chest. The others panted from fear and exhaustion. After a time, Jorry pulled himself to his feet.

"We made it," he announced.

"Not all," said one Quiplid, and the other added, "The Thanist fell."

26

"Bral, did you see it?"

The Skeggjatt gestured negatively, then gasped out, "Ran by him . . . to take the sledge. Didn't see . . . after that . . . didn't hear. . . ."

"He couldn't cry out," Jorry said, looking down on the massed stones that entombed Rull-Lamat.

"We saved the sledge," Axxal said. "All our equipment . . . safe."

Jorry went on as if he had not heard. "Rull-Lamat would have been able to figure out what's waiting for us. Without him, we're like blind men."

"Are you thinking of turning back?" Collen asked.

"Of course not," Jorry snapped. "We just have to be more cautious."

"Cautious? What good—will caution do us?" Bral blurted. "A planet where—where even the rocks are hostile—"

"One of the old stories about Boroq-Thaddoi mentioned a place called the Plain of Convergence. What it was, or where, no one could tell. I think that's what we just escaped," Jorry said.

"What else have you heard?" Collen asked.

"More than I want to think of. But in all the legends and tales, there's no mention of danger in the mountains. Once we reach them, we may be safe for a time."

"Then let's get started," the Quiplids said.

They reached the base of the mountains without further incident. By the time the dim sun had set and the long night was upon them, they had taken shelter in a shallow cave, stowed their gear safely, and lit a bright blaze at the entrance. At the end of their first day on Boroq-Thaddoi, seven were still alive. For this, they were grateful.

II.

The Mountain Camp:
Night and Morning

When their meal was done, the seven starfarers bowed to the long custom of wanderers at rest by a fireside, and began to talk. Only one topic could be considered. They all spoke of their plans for enjoying the treasure they hoped soon to possess. For a time, the hostile planet beyond the fire was almost forgotten.

"We'll hire ourselves a big man, bigger than Bral or Dolul, even," one of the Quiplids began.

"Won't hire him—we'll buy him, outright," said the other, who was perched on the rock shelf beside his brother.

"That's what we'll do, buy him outright!" was the gleeful response. "And we'll bring him back home, and fit him with a shoulder harness—"

"Like they wear on Az-Kef—"

"And he can carry us everywhere, one on each shoulder—"

"And everybody will have to look up when they want to talk to us!" the second Quiplid concluded, rocking from side to side in sheer exultation at the prospect.

"You'll each be able to buy your own stable of giants. Why do you want to share one?" Jorry asked.

"We stay close together," they said in unison.

Collen spoke up. "That's true of all you Quiplids. I don't believe I've ever seen a lone Quiplid in my life, always twos and threes, or more, in a bunch. Why is that?"

"When you're small, it isn't smart to be alone," said

one of the little men, and the other nodded solemnly in agreement.

"A sensible view, my friends. Very appropriate to our present situation. You've answered Collen's question and given us substance for meditation," Jorry said. "And what do you plan to do with your sudden wealth, Bral?"

"Go back to Verdandi and found a battle-school of my own. I'll turn out warriors to beat anything in the legends. The school of Bral will overcome anyone who stands against them in the tournaments."

"You did well in the last one yourself, I've heard."

Bral looked about proudly before saying, "I was the only survivor of my match. The medicos managed to patch a few others together, but only Bral walked off the field. It was a magnificent battle. Three hundred men in a fight to the death."

"Magnificent," Jorry murmured.

"I was credited with thirty-one kills, and I'll swear to two more. Men were gutted, dismembered . . . but they fought on, to the end."

"Very tenacious," Jorry observed.

"It was magnificent," Bral said once more. His eyes were bright, his voice husky with pride.

"So you've told us, twice. But really, now, Bral, what's magnificent about killing and dying for the amusement of paying spectators?"

"The warriors showed courage, eagerness for glory, fidelity to all the beliefs our people cherish. We treat the fallen as heroes and honor their names," Bral explained.

"What good is honor to a dead man?"

Bral looked at his captain half in anger, half in bewilderment. "That's all he has. That's all there is."

Collen broke the silence that followed Bral's words. "I'll get a driveship and seek out a good world to make my own."

"That's what I'm going to do," Axxal said. "I'll get a ship, the biggest one I can find—a whole fleet of them— and I'll take along all the Quespodons who want to go with me. We'll find a world where we can be the masters, instead of every other race's servants. We're not Skeggjatts, or Lixians, but we want honor and pride, too."

"Then don't listen to anyone from Old Earth this time," Jorry said, smiling faintly. "The pioneers gave your people poor advice at first contact."

"I know better now, Jorry."

Jorry turned to where Dolul sat, away from the fire, his back to the cold wall of the cave. "What of you, Dolul? What does an Onhla tribesman do with a planet's wealth?"

"Restore my tribe," Dolul said in a flat voice devoid of all emotion.

"Tell us about it," Jorry urged.

Very softly, Dolul answered, "No. It is not a thing to speak of."

An uncomfortable silence fell over the little group. Even the kiir birds ceased their clattering for a time. Beyond the travelers' sheltered niche, the wind shrieked and moaned over the barren rock, blustering each time it changed direction, as if seeking to drive the intruders out of hiding. The blaze of fuel blocks leapt and flickered and cast wild writhing shadows on the sloping walls. A sudden gust whipped the flame about and cast from outside a contemptuous sprinkling of grit into their midst. Then the wind died, and for a time, all was still.

Kian Jorry spoke into the silence. His voice was low and subdued, as of one thinking aloud. "Born under a calculating star . . . that's what they say about my people around the galaxy. And I do enjoy using my wits, that's true," he conceded, "but I'm not certain that it has anything to do with my blood. I've lived by my wits since I first set foot on the ramp of a driveship. My parents are long done with scheming, though I won't say as much for the rest of my kinfolk. No, my parents live one day at a time now, and take it as it comes. Fine folk. They pay their debts, speak well of their neighbors, and ask no more of the universe than their fair share." He fell silent, then sighed ruefully. "There's no reasoning with that kind when you're young. They're all sad faces and sincerity, a

30

homily every time they open their mouths, always at you to behave yourself. They love to see you settled down. Live a quiet life and die a quiet death, and when it's all done you can't tell one from the other. That's what drove me to the stars when I was little more than a boy. Can't say I regret it, either. I've been hungry more times than I care to remember, and my pockets were often empty. I've done my share of fighting, too . . . and my share of running. But I'll still take the starfaring life, risks and all."

Again he was silent, thoughtful, then he said, "When I first turned starfarer, I was a wild lad seeking adventure. A lifetime spent on solid ground was a desolate prospect to me. When Captain Crimmthann took me on, I looked upon him as my liberator. The old *Civility* had a rough crew on that first run, and I must have looked scared. The captain told me something I've never forgotten. 'Think what you will of freebooters, my boy,' he said, 'but the plain truth is this: At heart, every one of them is a farmer, or a merchant, or an innkeeper. Give them a good haul and they'll spend it all to buy themselves a safe berth among the groundworms.' I nodded my head, and said, 'Yes, sir,'—old Crimmthann would have cracked my skull if I'd dared to disagree—but I didn't believe a word of it. How could a man who's shaken the dust from his feet and felt the clutch of drivespeed in his guts ever go back to a groundling life? How can anyone return once he's looked back from out there and seen his homeworld as it is, a lonesome dust-mote lost in infinity?"

He stopped, but the others were accustomed to his rhetorical questions. They attempted no reply, and he soon went on, "Well, before long I found that I was wrong and old Crimmthann was right. On my third voyage, the *Civility* chanced upon a Triandal transport filled to bursting with cashcubes. I suddenly became a rich young man, rich enough to abandon my evil ways, buy three small ships, and start trading on my own. It's true, my friends. For a time, I was a legitimate businessman. Thanks to my heritage, I was a shrewd trader. And thanks to my early training, I knew how to avoid pirates. My goods always reached their destination. And so I prospered. I bought more driveships, and then more. Eventually I grew so prosperous that I no longer set foot aboard my own driveships; so very successful that I scarcely had time to eat, and no time at all for sleep. In fact, if I hadn't been reduced to beggary by a conniving partner—a solid, sensible groundworm—I would have been lost. But, thank the blazing rings, I was swindled and left with no more than the clothes on my back. And the *Seraph*."

They could not keep silent. "What did you do to him, Jorry?" asked one of the Quiplids.

"I walked away and let him keep everything," Jorry said. Noticing their expressions, he smiled and added, "Don't be so disappointed. It's true my people are not an affectionate race, but we don't approve of killing bloodkin. And it was my own brother who did me in. But I bore no grudge, and bear none now. I was free at last, and I knew what I wanted." Again he paused and looked around, as if to study the faces of his crew and search their minds. Then he said, "And if you wonder why I've decided to tell you this tale of my unsavory past, here's my reason. I'm disappointed in you. Soon every one of you is going to be richer than you can imagine, and all you want to do is settle down comfortably on a planet of your own and leave the stars to the likes of me."

"What's wrong with resting for a while, Jorry?" someone asked.

"Nothing at all, if that's what you want. I find it difficult to understand how anyone can want it."

"What do you want to do, Captain?" Bral asked.

"A great many things," Jorry said. He looked around the semicircle at his crew, drawing them in closer to attend his words. Even Dolul eased from his isolated post by the wall to join his shipmates. Jorry warmed his hands at the flame and spoke in a soft voice. "I want to go everywhere and see all the things I've heard of from crazy old spacerats—heard of and believed, even when everyone else laughed. If a thing can be imagined, then it exists out there somewhere. I have no doubt of it. And that will

32

be the beginning. Only the beginning. There are other galaxies out there, beyond the rim, and when I've seen all there is to see in this one, and done everything there is to do, I'll point the nose of the *Seraph* at one of those far galaxies and throw her into highdrive."

"But the *time,* Jorry. That would take a hundred lifetimes," Axxal objected, and Bral corrected him with, "A thousand, and more."

"All the more reason for me to hurry," Jorry said, laughing at their solemnity. "And all the more reason for my life-long interest in Boroq-Thaddoi. I'd have been tempted to come here anyway, simply to see and walk on a planet that frightened off so many starfarers and destroyed so many more. But the Leddendorf ransom made this place irresistible. With my share, I'll have the *Seraph* refitted. She'll go faster than anything else in the galaxy. Speed is the conqueror of time, my friends, and I'll have a ship to make time stand still."

"I've heard tales of starfarers coming home from a long trip and being younger than their children's children," Axxal said.

"The stories were true. Time is the enemy, but with a good ship for my weapon, I'll conquer that enemy. I won't just make time stand still for me, I'll make it run backwards. I'll go out there a creaking old man and come back a boy, ready to start over from the beginning."

All present had heard stories such as the one Axxal had mentioned, sad tales of far travelers returned to a home that had crumbled to dust, a family that had scattered, while drivespeed had softened for them the inevitable effects of time. They shared these melancholy stories until the long night reached its midpoint, and then Jorry ordered them to rest for an early start. He took the first watch alone.

Silence and solitude were old companions for Kian Jorry. He wrapped himself in a heavy cloak and huddled by the cave entrance, rifle across his knees. Beyond the glow of the fire, the wind moaned under a splendor of alien stars. Jorry gazed out, lost in his thoughts.

To him, thought was as real as action. He was a k'Turalp'Pa, descendant of the first civilized race encountered by the pioneers from Old Earth six centuries ago. Despite all his protestations of simplicity, he was typical of many of his people: a weaver of intricate plots, a lover of devious schemes, a man committed to subtlety and indirection in all his dealings. This trait was at once the strength and the greatest weakness of the k'Turalp'Pa. Their labyrinthine intrigues and grand designs for attaining power and wealth all too often came to serve as ends in themselves, and the intention took the place of the realization. To plan was a purer form of pleasure than to achieve. Supremely confident of their own contrivances, the k'Turalp'Pa too frequently fell victim to the unpredictable mischances of fortune. In such cases, their usual reaction was to curse the galaxy and all its residents, fall into a dark mood for a time, and then, having learned nothing, embark upon a new and even more ambitious plot. Such was their way, and it had made their homeworld a refuge for disappointed weavers of extravagant fancies.

Their world was a quiet world, a planet of peace, for the k'Turalp'Pa were not a strenuous people. They preferred to use the strength of their minds, and neglected the development of their bodies. In this respect, Jorry differed from them all. He had early learned that space was not a safe place for the weak or unready, and had hardened himself until he was now a match for anyone. Physically, he resembled the warlike Skorats, a kindred race, more than his own people. He did not boast of his strength, nor was he particularly proud of it. But he knew it was needed for survival.

Being a k'Turalp'Pa, he could not depend on strength alone, nor did he rest secure in cleverness. Concealed about his person were more than a score of Lixian finger knives. At close range, his aim was deadly.

In all their recorded history the k'Turalp'Pa had had no space flight nor any other form of aerial transportation. Their interests had always been artistic rather than scientific, and their accomplishments were considerable. It was the ancient k'Turalp'Pa who had perfected the motion painting, and an original work from that planet's great days was a priceless object on any civilized world.

When the first Earthmen came, the k'Turalp'Pa received them in peace and quickly absorbed all the newcomers offered. In the second great wave of migration, k'Turalp'Pa accompanied the pioneers. On many of the ships, they served as pilots.

But now, in the twenty-seventh century, k'Turalp'Pa were seldom seen off their homeworld. A rover like Jorry was a rarity among his people. And as he sat at his post, a dying fire and sleeping comrades to his back, cold and darkness before him, he thought of his home and his life and his long wandering, and was comforted. He had enjoyed successes, and survived failures; he had no regrets. Even the failures had been interesting. And his greatest success lay ahead.

The night was uneventful, and the wind fell with the fading of darkness. The crew of the *Seraph* rose and prepared their packs and once again loaded the sledge, working clumsily in the shallow cave. All were eager to be under way, but each was reluctant to be the first to step outside into the murky early light. Not until the sledge was packed, secured, and ready to move did one of the Quiplids venture past the embers of the night's last fuel block, on to the open mountain ledge. The others paid no notice to his departure until they heard him call out in a soft, almost childlike voice, "Jorry!" and then heard nothing more.

At the cry, Jorry, Bral, and Collen snatched up their rifles and raced from the cave. They saw no trace of their little companion. The barren rock of the ledge took no footprints, there was no blood, no sign of struggle, no hint of where the Quiplid had gone or what, if anything, had carried him off. He had vanished completely.

"Where is Jimm, Jorry?" the other Quiplid asked piteously. "What happened to him?"

"I don't know," the captain said, looking about him, up

35

the sheer mountain face, along the straight trail to the crest, down the long slope to the foothills. "Nothing could have taken him so quickly. It's not possible."

"But he's gone! You said there was no danger in the mountains, and now Jimm is gone!"

"I was wrong and Jimm was careless, and now he's gone. And that makes you very important to the rest of us," Jorry said, dropping to his haunches to bring himself almost to eye-level with the desolated Fimm. "I was counting on you and Jimm to get up over the outer wall and handle any locks we might encounter inside. It's all up to you, now. If anything happens to you, Fimm, we can't make it."

"What about Jimm? Can't we get him back?"

"How? We don't know what took him, or where he is. We can't even be sure he's alive. If we stay here, whatever took Jimm may take us, too. We have to move."

"Can't we look for Jimm? Please, Jorry."

"We can't risk it. I want you to ride on the sledge from now on. Stay where the man behind can see you." He placed a hand gently on the Quiplid's sloping shoulder, and said, "I'm sorry we can't look for Jimm, but we can't do it, and that's that, Fimm. We have to move on."

"All right, Jorry," the little man said. He walked to the sledge, waiting outside the cave entrance with Axxal harnessed to draw it, and climbed on the back, in Dolul's view. He sat there, unmoving, staring at the ground, a miniature embodiment of grief.

At Jorry's signal they started up the trail, to the crest of the mountains. The grade was shallow but unvarying, and Dolul and Axxal spelled one another twice before they reached the top.

Here the winds were strong and steady, and the prospect was limited only by the curvature of the small planet. A great open plain rolled unbroken to the horizon. The mountains continued on their right, curving around, becoming lower and less forbidding, ending at last in low hills and outcroppings of rock on the plain, as if the force that had thrust them up from the planet's interior had weakened and at last died here. To the left, a solitary mis-shapen mountain rose from the plain. Jorry pointed to it.

"That's the citadel," he shouted over the droning wind.

"It looks like a mountain," Collen said. "Are you sure?"

" 'A structure as big as a mountain, alone on the plain, dwindling hills hooked around one side,' " Jorry recited. "That's how it was described to me, and there it stands. Let's start down."

On a broad ledge, sheltered on both sides from the buffeting wind, they took their final rest of the downward journey. They were well past the halfway mark, and the surface of the plain, seen from a new perspective, revealed a scattering of odd shapes. One by one, the travelers turned their attention to these objects and voiced their wonderment.

Jorry ended their speculations with a word. "Ships."

III.

The Graveyard

From the base of the mountain they started across the open plain. Their progress was slow and exhausting. What had appeared a smooth firm surface turned out to be an expanse of soft sand that clutched at the heavy sledge and sucked at their feet as they trudged on.

The wind that had assaulted them at the upper levels was nowhere in evidence here on the plain. All was still, and no sound could be heard but the grating of the sledge-runners and the labored breath of everyone but Fimm, who maintained his solitary watch atop the mound of supplies. The group moved more and more slowly. When they reached a fallen driveship, not far from the mountains, Jorry signaled a halt. They sprawled in the sand, some against the sledge, others by the driveship, and for a time no one spoke. Jorry broke the silence.

"Now you can see why I didn't choose to land here," he said when his breathing was steady once more. "Bringing a driveship down on this would have been like landing on water."

"Why did they land here?" Bral asked, encompassing in a sweeping gesture of his big hand the driveships that lay, or stood at precarious angles, on the plain.

Axxal asked, "Yes, why, Jorry? Surely the pilots weren't fools."

"That's a generous statement," Jorry said, laughing. He was silent for a moment, then he admitted, "Truthfully, I don't know. Maybe the sand showed up solid on their instruments. Maybe they didn't feel like walking." He pulled off one boot, emptied the sand from it then re-

38

peated the operation with the other boot. "Can't say I blame them. This isn't the planet I'd choose for a leisurely stroll."

"I wonder what became of them," Axxal said.

"Forget about them. They're long dead, every one. This thing must be five centuries old, Galactic," Jorry said, indicating the driveship that curved its bulk over them and cast its shadow over the sledge and beyond.

"Is it really that old?" Axxal asked.

"Of course. Forward ports, raised bridge, external ramps, segregated drive components—you only find those on the ancient models. This must have been one of the first to leave the home system."

"She's been here a long time," Bral said.

Jorry agreed with that. He replaced his boots, stood, and approached the old hulk. The driveship was nearly ninety meters end to end. She lay on her belly, the forward portion buried almost halfway, the rear clear of the sand. Her plates were cracked and separated, the surface dulled and pitted with the dust of space, the sand and winds of Boroq-Thaddoi, and the passage of time. Her ports were cracked; some were completely shattered.

Near the midsection, a hatch stood open. Jorry looked at it for a time, until Bral's voice came to him.

"Going inside, Jorry?"

"I'm not here to explore old wrecks. Just indulging my imagination. There'd be little of value left in this heap."

The Skeggjatt had joined his captain, and now he gazed thoughtfully at the open hatch. "I wasn't thinking of valuables."

"What, then?"

"I'm thinking we might not have to go back to the *Seraph*."

Jorry shook his head decisively. "I'd sooner try to lift off in our sledge than one of these wrecks."

"This one may be past salvaging, but what about the others? Are they all wrecks?"

"There's nothing here in the *Seraph*'s class. We could

ring the galaxy in the *Seraph* in the time it would take to ready the best of this lot for takeoff."

Jorry's words carried clearly to the others, who rested by the sledge. Dolul listened attentively to the exchange, and then turned to Axxal. "Is Jorry right?" he asked.

The Quespodon considered for a time, and replied cautiously, "I think so. These old ships are tough, but such a long time unused . . . Wroblewski coils improve and strengthen with use. If they're idle for a long time, something happens to them. They lose power."

"So all these ships are useless."

"They're useless to us here and now. But if we had good mechanics, and tools, and heavy equipment, and new parts, we could repair one in a year or two. If we knew how to do the work. But there are six of us, and we have eighteen watches' food left. I don't like the thought of crossing the mountains and that valley again, but we have to if we want to leave this planet," Axxal said, sighing in resignation.

Fimm's voice, coming from the Quiplid's perch on the top of the sledge, startled them. "What about those other ones, Axxal?" he called. "Out there. Do you see?" Fimm pointed to the open desert that extended from the mountain range to the horizon. "That funny-shaped one, do you see it? And back there, in line with the sharp crag. What about that one?"

Axxal stared at one of the objects, then at the other, and averted his eyes with a shudder. His vision was not as acute as the vision of either the Quiplid or the Hraggellon, but he had seen enough and wished to see no more. One of the things—they could be nothing but driveships of some kind, but he was loath to apply that familiar name to such objects—was shaped like two squat pyramids joined near their apexes by long rods of varying thicknesses. The other was disturbing in a way Axxal could not explain to himself. It was a collection of pods joined by a webbing of slim columns; from the central, largest pod, something extended and seemed to disappear into itself. It resembled a helix, but its actual conformation was unlike any shape Axxal had ever seen or imagined. He shut his eyes and tried to force the after-image from his memory, where it writhed like something alive.

"What's the matter, Axxal?" Fimm asked.

"I don't like the look of those things. I never saw a driveship like them."

"Are they not Old Earth designs?" Dolul asked.

"No one from Old Earth ever made anything like those," Axxal replied.

Jorry and Bral had rejoined them by this time. Jorry shaded his eyes and looked out at the two strange constructions. He studied them for a time, but said nothing. Dolul repeated to him the question he had asked the Quespodon. Jorry was slow to respond.

"I'd sooner take my chances with this leaky old heap than set foot within a thousand meters of those things. They're the work of no race I'm aware of, and I don't care to meet their makers or see their handiwork too closely," he said at last.

"Maybe they're Rinn," Bral suggested.

"Maybe. No one's sure what the Rinn ships look like. But could they both be Rinn?" The question hung unanswered, and Jorry went on, "Maybe they're from outside." He seemed to think on his words for a time, and then faintly repeated, "From outside . . ."

"We'd better be moving, if we're going to reach the citadel by nightfall," Collen said.

"Yes, of course," Jorry agreed, distractedly, his attention still focused on the strange craft. "We have to hurry. Let's get moving."

Jorry was the last to take his place in the caravan, and he drew his eyes from the distant spacecraft with a reluctance obvious to all. As they stepped forward, Collen said to him, "You seem fascinated by those ships."

"They interest me, I can't deny it. If they *are* from another galaxy, there's no telling what I might find on them."

"You might find something you don't want," the Thorumbian said. "Unknown shapes from unknown stars

. . . I've heard stories about ships like that. They bring no good."

"If I knew for certain that they came from beyond the rim . . ."

"What if you did?"

"If they made it here, they can make it back. What better way to escape this galaxy?"

Collen stopped and stared at him. "You're talking like a madman, Jorry," she said in a cold, even voice. "Setting foot on an alien craft—even the sight of those things is unnatural!"

"Relax, my friend, and don't worry about old Captain Jorry's sanity. It's only a notion of mine. Intellectual curiosity. It keeps me from thinking of what may lie ahead," Jorry said.

They walked on in silence, bending all their energies to the effort of moving through the tenacious sand. The ruined driveships receded gradually. The citadel was still nearly half a day's march away, but even at this distance it jarred the imagination. It grew ever more awesome as they drew nearer, and drove all other thoughts from their minds.

It was impossible to determine at what point the natural rock ended and the work of the builders began, but intelligent planning and skilled workmanship were obvious in the upper reaches of the citadel. What staggered the mind was the purpose behind it. Some mad, brilliant architect might have dreamed this blending of the arts and materials of a hundred civilizations into a single monstrous edifice, but no known race could have erected such a thing.

The citadel of Boroq-Thaddoi was unique in the galaxy. It dwarfed the nine walls of Skix, the great corridor on Clotho, the ageless pyramids of Xhanchos, even the legendary cities of Old Earth in the proud and violent centuries before the exodus. It was the monument of giants.

Directly before the little band was a sheer rock wall that rose smooth and unbroken for two thousand meters to erupt in a fantasy of towers, turrets, and spires all joined by a web of arching ramps interlacing in a Gordian pattern of line and plane. To their left, the flat surface yielded to curving, rippling walls of polished black stone topped by a wide ledge that vaulted abruptly over a chasm to the rim of a truncated tower. To the right, the wall led into a series of what appeared to be titanic steps; beyond them extended great domes of crystal, and above them small domes of varied colors, and rising from these domes needlelike spires that soared to impossible heights before dropping in sharp angles to plunge to the towers all around them.

The variety of shapes and substances united in this single immense structure was enough to stir the consciousness of any observer. But as he approached the citadel, entered its shadow and sensed it looming over him, the observer would forget all else in wonder at the sheer mass of this sprawling, climbing, self-enveloping construction, a churning monstrosity of frozen stone, alone on a dead plain on an empty, shunned world.

Jorry and his band reached the base of the wall just as the faint sun slipped below the horizon. The sledge, emptied of its burden and raised at one end, served as rampart for their little encampment. That night Jorry posted a double guard. The second day had passed. Six were alive. The goal was within reach.

IV.

The Gateway

At first light they began to prepare their assault on the citadel. Three watches' food and water and the individual shelters were left, with the sledge, at the encampment. They would not be needed until the return trek to the *Seraph.* Everything else was to be carried.

Fimm, with a long line coiled over his shoulder, proceeded up the smooth wall, finding finger- and toeholds invisible to the others. His progress was rapid, and he soon reached a ledge that served as natural parapet to this fortress that was as much the work of nature as of artificer. He affixed the line securely and let it down for the next man.

Dolul was the first to follow him. Bral and Axxal were the next to ascend, each of them carrying, in addition to his own supplies, one of the kiir cages. Jorry followed, and Collen came last. When they were reunited on the ledge, Jorry reached into his tunic and withdrew a folded piece of metallic cloth covered with markings.

"Is that the map?" Bral asked.

"A kind of map. Can any of you read?" Jorry asked, laying out the document on the flat rock. As it developed—and as he had already determined—none of his crew had troubled to master the arcane and venerable art of reading letters, or of writing them. It was a rare skill in those times.

Jorry explained the mysterious markings for the others, concluding, "This is the summary of all my findings, along with my best-informed guesses. It's partly a map, partly a diagram, partly a listing of alternatives, and partly, I must admit, groping in the darkness of absolute ignorance. I have some idea of what to expect, and where to go, but there will be surprises. Be ready for anything."

"We are," Dolul said.

"Good. Fimm, haul up the rope and coil it on the ledge where we can toss it down fast. Leave it attached here. We may be in a hurry to go down." As the Quiplid set to his task, Jorry reviewed the others' rôles. "Dolul, you stay close behind me. If I signal, come up beside me on the right, and cover that field of fire ahead. Take Bral's rifle. Fimm comes next, with ammunition and spare lanterns. Then Bral and Axxal, and Collen guards the rear. If Collen gives the warning, Axxal supports her and Bral protects the supplies. Clear?"

Each one nodded. Jorry checked all weapons and then they began the march along the high ledge.

They proceeded for half the day, until they came to a point where the ledge turned sharply and led through a cleft into the rock wall. The way was dark, but a dim point of light showed far ahead. Jorry took one of the lanterns from Fimm and strapped it to his chest, leaving his hands free. He gave a second lantern to Collen.

"Exactly as before. Keep your marching order and be wary of everything," he said.

"We haven't seen anything yet," Collen said.

"Something took Jimm off."

The Thorumbian shook her head dubiously. "He could have fallen . . . a crevice in the rock. There's no food or water on the surface, Jorry—what could live here? How would it feed?"

Jorry grinned. "Your average starfarer, when properly prepared and seasoned, can be a tasty delicacy. Did you never think of that?"

"I've been thinking of it since we landed," Bral said.

"I don't say it's true, but let us be prepared. Perhaps Collen is right, and nothing lives on Boroq-Thaddoi but the poor fools who come in search of its treasure. But there are some references to an underground river, deep below the citadel, and creatures living in the darkness.

Maybe it's an old spacerat's nightmare, but let's not laugh it off. Everyone ready?"

They answered affirmatively, and Jorry stepped off into the dark narrow cleft that led to the mountain fortress. As he entered the passage, he switched on his lantern. For the first time since their arrival on this dim bleak world, the little group saw brilliant light. The stone walls blazed before them as Jorry opened the aperture to wide range and spread the beam of his high-intensity Kepler lantern over a hemisphere of shadowless radiance. The light cheered them, and they fell into place behind him. As Collen closed their file she switched on her own lantern, which she had affixed to her back. The little band walked through the darkness armored before and behind with the blaze of a sunside planet at midday.

Kepler lanterns were the best source of artificial light in the galaxy. Almost indestructible, they were highly prized on the homeworld, and strictly banned from trade. Jorry had obtained them only with great difficulty, of which he volunteered no details. They were essential to the success of his expedition, so he obtained them. He could be—as he sometimes reminded his companions—a most persuasive and resourceful man.

Twice in their passage to the interior they heard soft scraping noises high overhead, but when Jorry beamed his light upward, nothing was visible but the naked rock. They walked in silence, each one alert, and when they emerged onto an inner ledge that overlooked a deep natural amphitheater, relief was almost a tangible presence among them.

While the others rested, Jorry studied the open area below. The ledge spiraled around the inner wall, reaching the bottom after two complete circuits. Spaced irregularly along the ledge were openings into the encompassing wall similar to the one from which they had just emerged. He gave these a cursory glance, as if to assure himself of their existence as checkpoints, and turned his full attention to the floor of the crater. The short day was near its end and the faint light was waning. It was necessary for Jorry to turn the beam of his lantern downward and sweep the surface from side to side. At last he held on one spot, where a grid lay half buried in the sand. He chuckled with satisfaction.

"Take a look, my friends," he called to the others. "The nine doors, the gateway to the inner citadel. Somewhere beyond them the Leddendorf treasure is waiting for us."

"What else is waiting for us?" Collen asked.

"We'll find out when we've eaten and rested. Make camp here on the ledge. We'll shine a lantern in each direction, so one guard will be all we need."

"Are you sure, Jorry?"

"Positive, Axxal. We'll be working hard from here on. Everyone needs a good rest. A single guard is enough."

The Quespodon appeared unconvinced, but he did not argue the captain's decision. Jorry did not tell them of his belief that the number of guards made no difference at all to their survival. He wanted to foster confidence as they prepared for the most dangerous part of the mission. But he knew that if the hazards of Boroq-Thaddoi were one-tenth as grave as the old stories suggested, an army of guards would be of no more use than a pair of lanterns. He told himself that the stories were no more than stories. That night he slept soundly.

V.

The Sentinels

The floor of the crater was smooth and sandy. Jorry and Collen had extinguished their lanterns in the pale morning light, but as they drew closer to their objective, Jorry switched his beam on once more, focusing tightly on an upright object that was now visible near the grid.

"You've got the best eyes of us all, Dolul—what's that ahead? Some kind of marker?" he asked.

The Hraggellon studied the object for a moment and said, "No."

"Well, what is it?" Jorry asked impatiently.

"Not a marker. A plant."

"Something *alive?*"

"Yes."

They brought their weapons to the ready. As the form of the mysterious object became more distinct to all, they began to speculate, then to scoff, and at last, when they stood around it, to marvel. It was a living organism, a thick, dark-green stalk twice the height of Bral. From its top drooped three pendulous bloated leaves. As the starfarers drew closer in their encirclement, the leaves began to tremble faintly.

Jorry turned to Collen. "Apparently some things can live on this planet."

"How? What does it feed on?"

Jorry looked the plant over thoughtfully. He studied the base for a time, then, with the toe of his boot, he kicked away some loose sand. A few such passes and he had uncovered what appeared to be part of a rib cage. Collen and Bral knelt and assisted him, and in a short time they had uncovered most of a skeleton. The stalk was growing through the place where the belly had once been; it completely enclosed the spinal column and partially enfolded the lowest ribs with its outer bark.

"Now we know what it feeds on," Jorry said coolly.

In the silence that followed, Bral let out a sudden roar and threw himself on the plant. He clasped it tightly, set his feet wide, and slowly began to haul it from the ground. The leaves twitched and shuddered wildly at his first effort, then plunged down to strike clublike at his head. Bral hunched lower, ducked away from their wild flailing, and increased his effort. His face reddened, his breath labored loud, but at last, with a sound like the ripping of flesh, the roots of the stalk tore loose and a single shriek came from the plant as Bral flung it and the conjoined bones far from him. It had scarcely touched the ground before Dolul slashed it to pieces with quick scything strokes of his wrist blades. Bral stared at the ruin of the thing in silence, his chest heaving and his great shoulders trembling.

"Are you all right, Bral?" Jorry asked.

He looked at Jorry with vacant eyes. "It screamed."

"We heard. It's dead now."

"All around us . . . Seeds of those things may be everywhere, waiting for food. For *us!*"

Jorry's voice was firm. "We can handle them, Bral. We've proven that."

"Yes. We can handle them," Bral said, a bit more surely.

"We can overcome anything this planet sends against us. Remember that. This thing was a monstrous plant, but it's only a plant. Nothing more. We won't let ourselves be conquered by a plant." Satisfied that his words had had the desired effect, Jorry squatted beside the remains of the skeleton and said, "I want to take a look at this fellow. He might tell us something."

The broad, deep rib cage and spine were gone, but the rest of the bones lay undisturbed. Jorry lifted the skull and studied it with interest. It was a humanoid skull, very large, high-crowned, with a deep, heavy mandible. As he moved the skull, the lower jaw dropped slightly, as if in a grin. Jorry responded in kind.

"Fine set of teeth this fellow had. Great abundance of them, too . . . fifty-six, or I miss my count. He could take a good nip out of you, couldn't he?"

"What was he, Jorry?" Fimm asked.

"I haven't the slightest idea. I'm sure he was no Quiplid, at least," Jorry replied, replacing the skull and rising. "He's half again the size of Bral and Dolul, and his bones are as thick as Axxal's."

"A Lixian?" Collen suggested.

"No. Skull's the wrong shape, too many teeth. Lixians have an almost triangular skull and much frailer bones." Jorry stooped to clear the sand from what remained of the creature's hand. "Look there. Two flexible fingers and a triple-jointed thumb."

"I never heard of any race like that," Bral said.

"Nor have I. Our friend is from some undiscovered world, and a very advanced one, too. Or else he's from another galaxy. And he's a fairly recent arrival, to judge by the condition of his bones."

"Those ships—"

"By the blazing rings," Jorry said, awed by the sudden thought, "there may be scores of driveships on this planet, hundreds of them, all empty, waiting for crews that will never return! There's a thought to make us wary, eh?"

They reburied the skeleton and turned their attention to the grid. It consisted of three rows, each containing three low pyramids about four meters on each side and one meter high at the apex. A broad band of markings enclosed the base of each pyramid.

"How do we open them, Jorry?" Collen asked.

The captain laughed. "Very carefully. Only one of these is the proper entrance."

"And what if you open the wrong one?"

"I hope not to find out. I'm fairly certain which one we want."

Collen shook her head doubtfully. "It seems too easy

so far, Jorry. We walk through a passage, down a ramp, and here we are at the entrance. Where are all the obstacles?"

"Rull-Lamat and Jimm could tell you about obstacles, if you'd like. Have you forgotten so quickly?" Jorry gestured to the openings above them. "They're all blind leads, all but the one I took you through. If we had gone into the citadel, we could spend our lives wandering through it and never come near the entrance to the vaults. Old Captain Jorry thinks ahead, Collen, and that's why we got here so quickly. Trust me, and do as I say, and we'll come out of this healthy and rich."

Jorry walked slowly around the grid until he had studied it from all sides, then he consulted his map. He returned to one of the low pyramids and compared its markings with an entry on the map. Waving the others back, he stepped onto the structure and pressed on certain markings. When he reached the last marking on the fourth side, the pyramid began to rise smoothly, on four slim cylinders, until its base was head-high from the ground. Jorry retained his composure throughout. He dropped lightly to the sand and gestured to the opening with a triumphant flourish.

"Before we enter, let's make sure we can exit without embarrassing delay," he said. Pointing to a long stone imbedded in the sand some fifty meters off, a natural menhir broken from the surrounding ledge, he ordered Axxal, Bral, and Dolul to fetch it. When they returned with the slab, Jorry and Collen added their efforts to slide it diagonally under one corner of the door. "If this thing should decide to shut, we'll still be able to get out. I doubt that it has enough power to crush this chunk of rock," Jorry explained. Taking a coil of line from Fimm, he affixed it firmly to the stone and tossed it down. They heard its end strike, and when Jorry beamed a light down, they saw a corridor at the bottom of the shaft, not far below.

"There are handholds in the wall," Fimm pointed out.

"Let's trust to the line," Jorry said.

He led the way. The others followed in their marching order. At the base of the shaft they found themselves in a square tunnel of the same dimensions as the door and the shaft. The only light came from their lanterns, the only sound from their voices and movements. Jorry consulted his map, checked his weapons, and stepped off down the tunnel.

Three times they came to junctions where an identical tunnel intersected theirs. Jorry passed the first and second with little more than a glance, but at the third he paused, directed the beam of his lantern down each branch, then turned to the left.

Within a short distance, the appearance of the structure changed. The floor was as smooth and seamless as before, but the walls and roof were irregular, as if their way now took them through a cave left unfinished by hurried builders. Nor did this tunnel proceed in the straight line they had grown accustomed to; it zigzagged and meandered in its erratic natural course.

They proceeded for a long time, seeing no more branch tunnels, until Jorry abruptly called a halt. He unfixed the lantern from its straps, for greater precision of aim, and turned its light on a cluster of shiny globular objects that clung to the wall just above their reach. The things ranged from no larger than a man's thumbnail to almost the size of Fimm. Their exterior appeared hard. It shone in the lantern beam with the luster of polished metal.

"Does anyone know what these things are?" Jorry asked.

No one responded. Jorry swept the walls and roof with his beam, and other clusters reflected the light. The things looked harmless, but he meant to take no chances by trusting to appearances. As he stood deliberating, Fimm tugged on his boot top for attention.

"Look, Jorry," he said, his voice low and secretive. "One of them is coming to us."

A globule the size of Jorry's fist moved slowly down the wall and across the floor toward the Quiplid's feet. Jorry followed its progress, then flashed the beam around.

On all sides, by the hundreds, the things were silently moving toward them.

Jorry reacted quickly. Drawing and throwing in a single motion, he sent one of his knives into the globule nearest him. It burst silently upon contact, like a pricked bubble. A shiny substance glimmered on the floor of the tunnel where it had stood.

The other globules halted. Then, as if a command had been given, they began to dissolve, and the glistening filmy residue of their dissolution spread swiftly. As it flowed toward Jorry, he heard Fimm cry out and fall. At once he lost his own equilibrium; suddenly he seemed not to be standing on a floor of stone but on some slick and tractionless surface. He slipped, and the hand he thrust out for support slid from under him, causing him to fall heavily and lose his breath. The lantern skidded from his grip and spun across the floor until it clattered against a rock. There it lay, its beam directed at the roof of the tunnel, revealing great clusters of the globes, these larger, darker in color and dull-surfaced, all of them in motion, all crawling downward to where the invaders sprawled helpless.

For Fimm and Jorry were unable to rise, and could only writhe on the glassy surface. Bral, swinging his ax wildly, cleaved through a dozen of the globules at a stroke and fell with a crash as their fluid spilled forth under his feet. Dolul went down, then Axxal, and only Collen stayed erect, firing steadily into the massed objects above in the lantern's beam. They burst in a spray of droplets that fell with a crackling hiss on the rock around her and sent up wisps of acrid smoke.

Jorry cried, "Get the cages open—smash them if you must. But let the kiir out before those things from above can reach us!"

Collen lost her footing even as Jorry shouted, but she managed to kick the cages toward the others as she fell. Somehow, she kept up accurate fire. The cages careened across the tunnel floor. Dolul clutched at them and missed, but Axxal seized them. In frantic haste, he tore open the cages containing the kiir.

The little creatures burst angrily from their long confinement, their beaks clattering like clashing blades. They soared up into the lantern beam to get their bearings, then, ignoring the humans, they homed in on the bigger, duller globes, bursting them with merciless beaks and talons. For a brief interval, the six invaders were witnesses to a massacre, as the swift, vicious kiir swept like shot through the spherical things, Shrill bird-cries mixed with low mucid groaning. Then all sound faded and died as the round things fled into the darkness and the enraged kiir pursued them for the final kill.

All was silent for a time. Jorry called to his crew, and they answered him one by one. He and Dolul were bruised, and Collen had been burned by drops from one of the globules, but they were otherwise unharmed. With the immediate threat removed, the six worked their way beyond the slippery area and rested for a time.

"Lucky we had those birds," Bral said. "They went through the globes like . . . like . . ."

"Like true hunters," Dolul concluded approvingly.

"I hated the smell and the sound of them, Captain, but I'm glad you thought to bring them along," Bral admitted.

Jorry nodded. "Once, on Trigg-Embroe, I talked to an old spacerat who swore that a cage of kiir would have saved the men of the *Drake III*. He never mentioned the round things—I don't think he knew about them—but I decided then that when I came to Boroq-Thaddoi I'd bring kiir with me, just in case."

"If they hadn't driven them off, the ones from above would have dissolved us," Axxal said.

Collen limped to Jorry and sat down gingerly at his side. "Some of their juice got on my leg," she said. "Will you take a look at it? It burns."

"I'll have Axxal—" Jorry began. Collen broke in, "Not the Quespodon. You do it, Jorry. I want skill, not strength."

Under the lantern glare, the glistening blue-black skin

54

of Collen's calf and ankle was speckled with a dozen spots of dead gray where the fluid had spattered on her. Jorry cleansed the wounds and applied a salve, and with Collen attended to, they moved on.

They saw no trace, then or thereafter, of the globules or the kiir. The cavern went on a short way until it ended in a transverse tunnel running upward on their right and downward on the left. This tunnel, like the first one they had seen, was trimmed and finished on all surfaces. In addition, the walls wese ornamented with linear designs, curving, waved, or in parallel rows set at various angles. Jorry deduced that they were the marks of cutting implements, removed in the other tunnels but allowed to remain here for some unfathomable reason. The mere sight of something suggesting human workmanship was somehow reassuring after the things they had encountered.

Jorry took the downward branch. When they had marched for some time without a change in their surroundings, he placed the lead lantern in Dolul's care and went to check Collen's injuries.

He fell back slowly, pausing to speak a few reassuring words to each of his band. Fimm was emerging from his initial deep sorrow at the loss of his brother, and Jorry consoled him with a vivid description of the monument they would erect to Jimm's memory when they were all rich and far from this malevolent world. Leaving the Quiplid in improved spirits, he passed on to Bral. The big Skeggjatt, having confronted two enemies and overcome both, was much emboldened. Axxal was no more nor less fatalistic than usual. A Quespodon seldom anticipated the best.

With a final cheering word to Axxal, Jorry paused to wait for the last of their number to reach him. The burns on her leg had slowed Collen. The bobbing light of her rearward lantern lagged far behind the rest of the band. With each step the others took, the Thorumbian fell farther in the rear. Jorry called a halt at once, and the others sat or sprawled to await their companion.

Jorry leaned his back against the cool surface of a

smooth and unadorned stretch of wall. On either side of him, the wall was covered with linear designs: ahead, a rippling wave pattern; behind, narrow, close-set parallel lines. He pondered the reason for the markings, puzzled over their possible function, but could arrive at no explanation.

"Collen is slow. Her leg must be bad," Bral called to him.

"It didn't look like much. Just a few small burns."

"Digestive juices, Axxal," Jorry said. "The pain must be considerable. I'd gladly give her something to ease it, but that's too risky. We need Collen fully alert. Fortunately, the first thing a weapons master learns is self-control."

"Are digestive juices really that powerful?" Axxal asked.

Bral mumbled something about typical Quespodon stupidity. Jorry ignored the comment and said simply, "If that second wave of globules had reached us, we'd all be liquefied by now."

"What if we run into more of them? The kiir are all gone."

"In that case, we'll trust to our weapons and to Collen. She was doing well with her rifle, even before the birds were free. Next time, we won't be taken by surprise."

They turned toward the Thorumbian, who was now close at hand, her form outlined in the glow of the lantern strapped to her back. Her silhouette bristled with weaponry. Jorry took the lantern, narrowed the beam, and shone it on Collen's path.

"Don't rush, Collen. We're waiting," he called.

"I'll be with—"

Her words were cut short by a hiss that dulled at once into a muffled grating, then silence. A bright blur seemed to flash before the eyes of the five watchers. When their vision cleared, Collen's lantern was out. Her slender form, in the steady light of Jorry's beam, was somehow misshapen. Then, as they stared in uncomprehending horror, the Thorumbian disintegrated and slid to the ground. She had been slashed into wafer-thin sections by blades that flicked from the walls to shear unhindered through flesh and bone and metal.

VI.

The Door and the Jewels

"Hold your ground!" Jorry commanded, flinging his arms wide to keep his companions from rushing to the gory mound that was Collen's remains.

"I'm not afraid of plants or those round things. I can fight them, Captain. But machines . . . Collen had no chance."

"Would you have us turn back, Bral?"

"No. I don't know. How can we go on?"

"How can we turn back?" Jorry countered. "Whatever set off those blades may be waiting to do the same to anything that passes through from now on."

"The same thing might be ahead."

"It might be ahead. We *know* it's behind us. We have to go on."

They resumed the march at once. Collen was left where she lay. Axxal, equipped with the spare lantern, now took the post of rear guard. Jorry's decisiveness had restored them somewhat, but the shock of Collen's death kept them silent for a long time.

Jorry mildly regretted the loss of a shipmate. He was far more grieved to lose the little expedition's defender and all her weaponry. Only five of them remained now, with their personal arms and two rifles. Still, they were close to their objective; Jorry felt sure of that. Distances were uncertain, and terrible things might await them; but others had gotten through somehow, and escaped to lift off. They could overcome, if they did not weaken.

Far ahead, something glinted in the lantern beam. As they advanced, it divided and redivided and at last resolved into a pair of massive gates covered with a scrolled design of bright metal, inset with stones of various shapes and sizes and all imaginable colors. They studied the structure appreciatively, and Jorry pointed out gaps in the lower portion of the door where stones had apparently been pried from their settings.

"Someone's been here before," he said.

"The men from the *Drake?*" Axxal asked.

"Perhaps." Jorry counted the sockets. "Twenty-six. That's something like the number of stones found on the crew of the *Drake.* Well, I'd say this is an encouraging sign. We know that someone came this far and got out again, and into space."

"But they were all mad."

"We don't know what happened aboard the driveship, Bral."

"No. You're right. But, look, Jorry . . . isn't it possible that this is the treasure, right here? We could take the stones and start back now."

Without a word, Jorry handed his rifle to Axxal, drew his knife, and set to work to prize one of the stones free. When he had done so, he tossed the jewel carelessly to Bral. "Take it. With that, you can buy yourself a good-sized driveship or a battle-school and trainers. Is that enough for you?"

"If we stripped the doors . . ."

"We'd be very wealthy men," Jorry conceded, "but we would have settled for less than we've earned. Are you forgetting that three of our companions have died for the Leddendorf ransom? *That's* what we're here for. Not a pocketful of stones, but every bit of treasure we can load on our backs." When no one responded, Jorry softened his tone and went on, "However, just in case we run into difficulties up ahead, it might be prudent to collect a few choice specimens. Fimm, you have nimble fingers—pluck out a few stones for each of us, will you?"

The jewels flashed and glittered in the lantern glow, and their inner fire seemed to flow into the hearts of Jorry's crew, suffusing them with new courage. The sight of such opulence, the sleek feel of the heavy gems between their fingers, the thoughts of what they would bring, rekindled the starfarers' determination. When Jorry ordered Fimm to unlock the gates, they were all eager to press on.

It took the Quiplid some time to locate the locking mechanism and decipher its workings, but he succeeded at last. Slowly and silently the gates opened inward upon a broad, high chamber. Jorry flashed the light inside, where it illumined a wide floor, thick with dust in a cover undisturbed for ages. Nothing had passed through this chamber since the gate was sealed. He swung the beam in all directions, and started back. On both sides and before them were tiers of human forms.

In a moment Jorry recovered from his surprise. He opened the lantern to its widest range and turned it once more on the rows of silent spectators, then he announced, "They don't move. Either they're statues or they're all dead. Come on. If one of them *does* move, shoot it."

The chamber was utterly still. Deep dust muffled their footsteps and the cool dry air seemed to absorb the sound of their breathing. They walked out on the open floor until they were near enough to the lowest tier of figures to touch them. Only a low barrier of carved stone separated the invaders from the silent watchers.

The creatures behind the barrier were long dead. They were slightly smaller than Jorry, slender, with humanoid features. Robes hung in shreds from their bony frames. The skin was as dry leaves on the lolling skulls and dangling forearms. Wherever Jorry turned the lantern, the beam revealed the same sight: a silent patient audience of grinning dead.

"What happened to them?" Bral whispered.

"I don't know. They look as if they just took their places here and died."

Axxal glanced about nervously. "What is this, Jorry? Are we in a temple?"

"It could be anything. A theater, a hospital, a courtroom . . . maybe a tomb. Maybe this is how they buried their dead."

Dolul spoke. "No. All died together."

"How do you know?"

Dolul groped for a word to express something he had learned among the semihuman predators of Hraggellon, but no word for this sense existed. "I know," he said. "I can sense it."

"I'll not debate the point. Let's find the way out."

They walked up a long ramp, between rows of dead all facing the gates through which the five had entered, and came at length to a second pair of gates, these as massive as the others but plain and unadorned. Again, Fimm directed his skills to the lock. It yielded to him more quickly this time.

The Quiplid dropped to the floor as the doors swung slowly toward them. With a clatter and a flicker of dry white bone in the lantern beam, the upper portion of a skeleton fell inward. Legs and pelvis lay unmoving where they had lain for unknown ages. Skull and rib cage rocked languidly at Jorry's feet.

"Another of those big fellows we found up above," Jorry announced. Stooping for a closer look, he stilled the rib cage with his fingertips and pointed to three ribs whose ends were fused and rounded, as if by intense heat.

Axxal's powerful hand gripped his shoulder. "Look, Jorry. Another one," he said, pointing down the tunnel to one more sprawl of bones.

The second skeleton lay face down. A long dagger with a twisted handle intruded deeply between two upper ribs and emerged for a third of its length just below the humped shoulder blade. The two spinelike digits of its right extremity were tightly curled around the twisted grip of a dull metallic tube. Jorry eased the tube free, inspected it, and then motioned the others to step aside. He aimed the tube at the skull of the first creature. A sharp snapping sound came from the tube and a ball of white flame hissed forth, burning cleanly through the dead bone. Looking around at the others with great satisfaction,

Jorry thrust the new-found weapon into his belt, then stooped and yanked the blade from the skeleton's ribs.

"You need a good blade, Axxal," he said, tossing it to the Quespodon. "Take it as a memento of our overgrown friends. Whatever world they hail from—in whatever galaxy—they act much like all the humans I know. I'm not sure whether I should be encouraged or disappointed."

"Then they killed each other!" Fimm cried.

"I think that's a reasonable conclusion. Shouldn't be at all surprised to come upon a few more of these creatures, similarly done in."

"But why?"

"Did they go mad, like the crew of the *Drake?*"

"Did the one at the grid have anything to do with it?"

Jorry raised his hands to halt the flood of unanswerable questions. "The fellow we met up above had nothing to do with these, I'm quite sure. His bones were fresh— these are ancient. As for your other questions, we may never know. But it's important to remember that these two killed each other. The planet didn't kill them. All we have to do is stay together, and we'll win out."

In a low voice, Axxal asked, "Then who killed the one at the grid?"

Jorry frowned thoughtfully, then he shook his head and laughed. "I'll tell you that when I figure it out. Let's move on."

Jorry's prophecy was fulfilled at the first turning of the corridor, when they came upon more of the elongated skeletons. These bore no marks of violence, and yet they were twisted into grotesque contortions. Unlike their companions, whose garments—if they had worn any—were long fallen to dust, these each had a covering over the skull: a dry, dull, sand-colored mask fitted tightly to the bone.

"Just as you said, Jorry," Axxal murmured.

"Yes. I wonder what those facemasks . . . maybe these were the slaves. I've never seen . . ."

Axxal and Bral bent over the skeletons, and in a motion of terrifying swiftness, two of the masks twitched free and hurled themselves at the starfarers' heads. Axxal flung his arms before his face, and the thing affixed itself skin-tight to one forearm, but Bral did not move fast enough to save himself. Like the skulls before him, he was encased in a tight mask from chin to nape. He clawed at it wildly, staggered, and went to his knees. He climbed to his feet, then fell again and writhed silently on the floor of the tunnel, crushing and scattering the heaped bones.

Meanwhile, the masks had slipped from the remaining skulls and were moving across the floor in swift undulations to attack Jorry and Dolul. Jorry drew the tubular weapon. He tracked the fluttering form as it closed in, and fired. It blazed with a foul oily smoke as the fireball struck, and its companion halted long enough for Jorry to score a second hit.

By this time, Axxal had succeeded in tearing the thing from his forearm. It had not been able to interfuse with that leathery skin. He stood panting, grunting with pain as the blood oozed from his forearm. The thing he had ripped from him, its color now much darker, lay still for a moment as if stunned, then began to lurch away. Jorry took it with a careful shot, then turned to Bral.

The Skeggjatt lay motionless, fingers clawed deep into the mask that now shone a bright liverish-brown and pulsed with fresh life. Jorry burned the thing away with a final shot. He turned the lantern beam on Bral, and quickly averted it from the big man's corroded features.

"Away from here, fast," he said.

No one disputed the order. With Jorry leading, the four walked on. They stayed closer together now, and each carried a weapon in his hand.

They came without incident to the end of the tunnel. Before them, a shaft opened. It was about five meters from side to side. When Jorry leaned over and turned the light downward, a faint glimmer returned from below.

"Down there is the place of the columns, and somewhere among them is the vault where Leddendorf's treasure is hidden. We're almost there," Jorry announced.

"We've lost four men," Axxal said.

"I regret that as much as you do, but I can't change it. Let's be sure we lose no more."

"How can we be sure? This place, everywhere we look, everything in it . . . it's a monstrous world!"

Jorry's tone was impatient, as if he were talking to a complaining child. "Of course it is. No one goes to a Q-world to enjoy the scenic beauties and the climate. Relax your guard for an instant, and you're lost. Maybe Collen couldn't have escaped the blades, but the others might still be alive if they'd been cautious. We're taking a big chance being here, but the prize is worth it. If we're careful, and we stick together, Boroq-Thaddoi won't get us."

Once again, despite even the fresh memory of a ghastly death, Jorry's words rallied them. He called a brief halt, and while the others ate, he cleaned and dressed the raw patch on Axxal's forearm. This done, he inspected their location carefully, and evaluated the situation. All in all, it seemed the suitable time and place to rest and renew their strength for whatever might await them on the lowest level. He set the lanterns to illumine the rim of the shaft and the tunnel behind them, and told the others to rest while he stood watch. Fimm, protesting wakefulness, begged for the first watch, and Jorry yielded without argument. He stretched out on the floor and went to sleep at once.

The next thing he was aware of was Fimm's frantic voice in his ears, the little creature's fists drumming on his shoulder. He sat up, and was at once aware of a growing roar filling the tunnel.

"Something's coming, Jorry! Something's after us!" the Quiplid cried frantically.

The others were awake by now. Looking back in the direction they had come, they saw a thin dark line jerking toward them in the very center of the tunnel. Its progress was accompanied by an ever-swelling roar, like slow brutal footsteps.

The walls were coming together behind them.

64

VII.

The Place of the Columns

At Jorry's order, Fimm snatched the forward lantern and slipped over the rim of the shaft. Axxal and Dolul followed. Jorry stood at the edge, lantern in hand, until the others were safely started down, then he lowered himself quickly to a solid foothold. He affixed the lantern to his back and dug his fingers into the crevices at hand. Over his head the walls crashed together with a final roar that reverberated through the shaft. The impact jarred fingers and toes in their desperate grip on the rough walls and sent fragments of stone clattering down around the four.

When the last echo had died, and the air was still, Jorry called, "Is everyone safe?"

They answered one by one, and at each voice, Jorry shone the lantern on the speaker. He turned it upward then, and above their heads the beam reflected off a solid ceiling of rock with a thin seam down its center. Jorry gave the word to start down.

"How can we make it?" Axxal asked desperately. "We'll never be able to climb that far down."

"We can't go back up, and we can't stay here. Let's get started. Fimm first."

The downward climb was slow and difficult. The rough walls afforded good hand- and footholds, and Fimm picked out the easiest way for his companions to follow, but the descent seemed endless. As they dropped lower, the sound from below, faint at first, increased in volume until it was a roar that drowned out all but the loudest shouts. Jorry turned the beam down and they saw a rushing current.

"What will we do, Jorry? It may be a long way to land," Fimm called to him.

"Then we'll swim."

Axxal asked, "How will we get back up?"

"We won't. No race in the galaxy builds a house without a back door. We'll find the back door. Stop worrying, all of you. We're rich already, and we'll soon be richer."

At the end of their descent, they found to their great relief that one bank of the underground river was almost directly under the shaft. They dropped to it, set up the lanterns, and took a long rest.

"Well, now. We didn't even get our feet wet. Maybe our luck is changing," Jorry said brightly.

"Maybe it is," Axxal said, sounding unconvinced. Fimm added his agreement.

Dolul said nothing. His senses were alert, probing into the darkness deep beyond the lantern glow, reaching out for lifesigns.

The waters flowed swiftly past them. On each bank, a smooth pavement extended back some ten meters, then ended. Beyond this point, the floor was rough-hewn rock. Here began the columns.

They stood at regular intervals, about three meters apart, four meters high, and extended as far as the eye could see. The movement of their shadows in the shifting light of his lantern was a sight not to Jorry's liking. He did not repeat it. He crossed to them, inspected one column closely, then a second, and then many more, seeking some pattern to their construction and placement. He could find none.

The columns were infinitely varied. Some had clearly been cut by a primitive hand from a single block of stone; others were constructed ingeniously of several irregular blocks fitted together; still others seemed to be natural formations, stalactites reaching down to fuse with stalagmites into a single pillar of slow-growing stone that somehow retained the dimensions of the artificial columns. Which had come first, he could not tell.

He found some columns of a blue-green metal, warm to

the touch; some of a creamy stone so soft and porous that his fingers left indentations on the surface; here and there were some made of a material he had never seen. Some bore bright markings or deeply incised inscriptions in unfamiliar characters; most were unadorned. Wherever he looked, Jorry found no two exactly alike.

He turned from the puzzling structures and rejoined his companions, who had stayed by the bank. "The vault is on this level," he told them.

"Where?" Dolul asked.

"My very question. I had hoped that Rull-Lamat would assist us at this point, but that is no longer possible. Now we may have to do a bit of hunting. That's your specialty, isn't it?"

"Does the map not say?"

"It does not. Actually, all I have to go on now is the dying rant of a madman, related at thirdhand by a space-happy old drifter."

"Are we lost, Jorry?" the Quiplid asked.

"No. We sought the place of the columns, beneath the citadel. Here it is. We have to do some searching, that's all."

Dolul said, "You are the leader. Lead us."

From behind the glare of his lantern, Jorry studied the big tribesman. Dolul was speaking more now than he had during the long voyage, and Jorry did not like what the Hraggellon was saying. He sensed trouble ahead, but he answered pleasantly, "Quite right, my friend. I must accept my responsibilities. Good of you to remind me."

Hraggellons were unaccustomed to the subtleties of human speech. Nevertheless, Dolul sensed the edge in Jorry's words. Warnings had been exchanged. He accepted all without expression. Jorry and the others soon would trouble him no more. He could already perceive the beings converging on them from the encircling darkness.

The lantern flicked aside and columnar shadows swooped eerily in its path. Dolul's slitted pupils dilated at once, and he swept their surroundings with a searching glance. Nothing could be seen, nor was anything yet to be heard, but Dolul had other sensory resources. He was aware of swift strong figures gliding toward them, smoothly making their sightless way through the labyrinth of pillars to home in on the glimmering bright intrusion. He concentrated on the creatures, probing for their essence. These pale inhabitants of the lightless places were fierce, and the presence of aliens provoked them to destructive rage. But they lacked a leader. They could be dominated, Dolul sensed, by a single strong mind.

Dolul weighed his discovery. For one who had wrested to himself the leadership of a hunting pack, gaining mastery over the creatures of Boroq-Thaddoi should prove simple.

Jorry held the beam on the pavement, raising it to shine far ahead of them. "We go this way," he said.

"Are there any guardians?" Axxal asked.

Jorry threw a circle of light around them before answering. "I've heard tales. I don't know if they're true or not. If anything lives down here, there can't be many of them, and I suspect that our best weapon will be the lanterns."

"What about the rifles and sidearms?"

"I'm not suggesting that we throw the rest of our weapons into the stream, Axxal," Jorry snapped, "but it occurs to me that a race that's lived in total darkness for a few millennia would be mighty disconcerted by the beam of a Kepler lantern, full power, directly on the spot where they once had eyes. I'm thinking they'd be quite sensitive to powerful light."

Axxal grunted his assent. Dolul, in shadow, heard and silently agreed. He had perceived the creatures' apprehensions.

Jorry placed the Hraggellon at their rear, assigning him the second lantern. Axxal, with the other rifle, stayed just behind Jorry, and Fimm hurried along behind him.

Dolul felt the guardians drawing closer. A cluster were ahead, two or three among the pillars on their flank, far back, still out of sight. Some were approaching on the other side of the stream. He sensed none behind them. He had anticipated their sensations of anger and curiosity, and was surprised to find that they also emitted a growing fear.

Suddenly all emanations of fear ceased, and Dolul received a great surge of fury from the creatures. They had analyzed the intruders, and judged them to be easy prey.

Dolul's confidence was shaken. He had never before sensed a destructive urge of such intensity. He had known tormagons, who killed for food and hunting grounds; he had lived among men, who killed for pride and power; but these creatures killed simply because they found other life forms intolerable. Not even he could dominate such ferocity. His half-formed thoughts of betrayal were swept from his mind while Dolul focused all his powers on locating and counting the guardians. There were many of them, moving swiftly, converging. He received another overwhelming sensation of hatred, and shouted to the others, "They are coming! The guardians are on all sides!"

Before his last words, something sprang from the darkness and fastened itself on Fimm. Dolul decapitated it with a single slash, but too late to save his little crewmate. The Quiplid had been killed before he had time to draw his blade.

Jorry fired twice, then cried, "The lantern, Dolul—put it before you and turn it to full power. We'll stand back to back and fire on everything we see."

"How many are there, Jorry?" Axxal asked.

"Two less than when we came."

"Three less," Dolul corrected him.

"Good. That might be enough to drive them off."

"No. They must destroy all who enter their ground. I can feel their hatred. They will attack as long as one survives."

"That simplifies matters considerably," Jorry said. "We'll kill them all, and seek the ransom at our leisure."

"They are many."

"We've got plenty of ammunition, and at this range we don't have to be marksmen. Let them come."

They were silent for a time, listening, then Dolul said,

"They come." Soon the three starfarers heard soft rustling movement all around them. Jorry swung his lantern in a semicircle and it fell on two crouching figures who sprang back into the shelter of a column at the touch of light. They moved swiftly, but Jorry had a glimpse of them.

"It is as you say. The light causes them pain," Dolul said.

"Glad to hear it. By the rings, they're ugly. All jaws and teeth. And stench."

"They look strong," Axxal added.

"I'm sure they are. But I saw no weapons, which means that we're stronger. What are they up to now, Dolul?"

"They are preparing to attack."

"Give them a dose of the lantern. I'll do the same. That ought to throw their timing off. Axxal, if the light shows anything, fire."

Jorry raised his lantern and turned the beam to his left. It fell full upon one of the creatures moving in on them. The thing reared backward, throwing one taloned hand over its face and lashing out wildly with the other. Axxal's shot caught it squarely in the chest, slamming it back against a pillar, where it slumped and settled to the ground. Jorry held the light on it, fascinated by the fungoid white of its matted pelt, the flaring ears that rose above and beside the flattened eyeless head, the wide nostrils, and the bristling fangs.

Axxal fired twice more, in the direction of Dolul's beam, before Jorry moved his lantern. The light fell on others, who snarled, covered their eyeless faces in atavistic instinct, and lunged for the sheltering darkness of the columns. Jorry set the lantern down and, as he spoke to the others, drew the tubular weapon from his belt.

"Listen carefully. I want each of you to fire a dozen fast rounds straight ahead, into the lighted area. Then turn to your left and close your eyes until—"

"Close our eyes?!" Axxal blurted.

70

"I'm going to get us more light, and I don't want you both blinded or you'll be useless. Do as I say."

They did as Jorry directed. He aimed the tubular weapon into the unlighted sector on his right, closed his eyes, and fired. Turning quickly to his left, he repeated the action. Fireballs of white light hissed into the blackness. As each smashed against a column, it erupted into a burst of flame that glared bright orange even through Jorry's tight-shut lids.

As the light faded, he gave the order to fire. The creatures were staggering, clutching at their faces, emitting awful cries and snarls at the agonizing presence of the hated light. Jorry, Dolul, and Axxal pumped their fire into the helpless figures until the last embers of the fireballs had died and only the lantern light remained.

"We got a lot of them," Axxal said.

"More will come," Dolul told them.

Jorry laughed. "We'll get them, too. I'll give the rest of these a chance to think over what's happened, then I'll use the firetube again. Whoever those big fellows were, they knew the right weapons to bring."

"But they all died."

"Maybe not, Axxal. We only saw the ones left behind. I think the rest escaped."

"Did they take the treasure?" Axxal asked, dismayed.

"No. They came and left long before Leddendorf's time. They came for something else. The ransom is still here, and we'll have our hands on it as soon as we've disposed of these ugly beasts. Get ready—I'm going to use the firetube again."

Two more fireballs burned into the darkness. This time, one splattered against a column of soft stone, dislodging a sizable chunk of it, and the other burst against one of the warm metal pillars, which ignited and blazed with furious intensity. The cries of the guardian beasts silhouetted against the glow of the burning pillar became howls of helpless rage as the starfarers gunned them down.

"They can't take much more," Jorry said as he reloaded. "We must have killed fifty of them."

71

"I sense . . . indecision. Some want to stay. Destroy us. Others say to leave," Dolul said.

"I'll settle the dispute. Ready?"

Before Jorry could fire, guardians rushed upon them from the darkness of the left flank. Dolul shouted a warning, but his words were choked off by the two who hurled themselves at him, one fastening on his throat. The Hraggellon's rifle clattered to the ground. Axxal took the brunt of the next attacker's rush, seized him by the neck and thigh, and hurled him against a column. The splintering of bone was followed by the loud crack of the stone. Jorry sent a burst from the firetube into the midst of the attackers. They fell back, and he fired to the other side, then sent fireballs hurtling in every direction. All around them, columns went up in flame, or cracked and splintered from the waves of heat. The cavernous spaces lit up with a daytime glow, and Jorry sent fireballs one after another into the figures that scurried for shelter on every side.

The flaming metal pillars gave off a loud, hollow-roaring drone that grew louder as the flames spread. Behind this sound, Jorry heard another, deeper rumble. He fired one last time, then paused and waited for the distant echoes to fade. Instead, the rumbling grew, and came nearer.

Dust and chips of stone fell from overhead. A column collapsed near at hand, and a great slab of stone dropped from the roof, followed by a clatter of loose rubble. Jorry turned to Axxal. The Quespodon stood wide-eyed, a rifle in either hand.

Then something heavy crushed him to the ground, and Jorry knew no more.

PART TWO:

To the Pyramids

I.

The Tale of the Trickster

Jorry regained his senses aboard the *Seraph*. His head ached, and he felt the desperate thirst that follows a zaff-induced sleep. He tried to rise, but bandages tightly enclosing his ribs immobilized him. He could remember nothing after the dark vaults, the attacking pale things, the roaring . . . and now he was back on his ship. He worked his slow and uncomfortable way to a half-sitting position and bellowed for Axxal, who came at once.

"Get me something to drink, quickly," Jorry croaked. When he had gulped down the water Axxal gave him, he wiped his lips and demanded, "Now, tell me what happened. Go ahead, tell me everything. I want to know."

"The vaults collapsed. It must have been the noise of the firing that did it. Dolul once told me that on Hraggellon, his people cause ice and snow to fall from the peaks by making loud noises, and in the vaults—"

"Yes, yes, I know. I must have lost my head for a time there. The sight of that thing within arm's length of me. . . ." Jorry shuddered, and was silent for a moment before asking, "But how did we escape?"

"I found the way back to the sledge and gave you all the zaff solution we had left. It kept you quiet and eased the pain. I left the sledge behind. I carried you back myself in a single day. Your ribs looked bad, and I didn't think you could afford an extra day without care."

"They hurt badly enough," Jorry admitted. "Did you bind them up?"

Axxal nodded proudly.

"Well done. Your talents exceed my hopes, Axxal. And

75

how did you get us out of the citadel with the shaft blocked and the vaults collapsing all around us?"

Almost beside himself with pride now, the Quespodon smiled and said, "I found the back door."

"Would you clarify that a bit, please?"

"Remember, when we were climbing down the shaft, you said that no race in the galaxy builds a house without a back door? When everything started falling, I thought of the back door. It had to be the stream. All that water had to go somewhere."

"Of course. Very sensible of you. And where did it go?"

"To a valley behind the citadel. A green valley, Jorry, with trees and plants."

Jorry's expression changed to disgust. "More of those flesh-eating monstrosities like the one at the grid?"

"No, Jorry. Nothing like that," Axxal said excitedly. "Real trees and plants. Edible fruit and good soil. And the valley was sheltered from the wind. It was just like an ordinary world."

"Hardly, Axxal. But you got us out. That's better thinking than I'd expect from a Quespodon."

"I can think, Jorry. I'm not like the others."

"Don't be touchy, my boy. Quespodons are not famed throughout the galaxy for intellectual achievement, and you know it. Of course you can think. If you couldn't, we'd both be dead."

"Like Fimm and Dolul," said Axxal. "Those beasts got them both."

Jorry looked away, silent and frowning, for a time. He weighed the information. "I always had my doubts about Dolul. He spoke the common tongue, like the rest of us, but he spoke the language of beasts, too. I was never sure which was his true language."

"Hraggellons are human," Axxal pointed out.

"Humanity is more than a matter of appearance. Dolul was in mental contact with those creatures. He knew how they felt, he could sense it. But still, they got to him. . . .

76

Maybe it was a mistake to enlist him. The Onhla tribesmen never did get on with other races."

"Why did you bring him, if you doubted?" Ordinarily, Axxal would not have dared ask such a question of his captain, for Jorry was not one to accept inquiry. When he chose to confide in someone, he spoke freely, but not quite frankly; on any occasion, he told just what he wanted to tell, and no more. He did not explain himself, nor did he offer justifications. But Axxal sensed a change in his captain, and he took advantage of it.

Jorry answered him bluntly. "I needed an Onhla for this job. I picked my crew carefully, Axxal. Not because I liked them—because they could do a particular job that had to be done. That was my only criterion."

"Why did you take me along?"

"I needed a strong man I could trust."

Axxal hesitated, then said, "And you picked a Quespodon because you don't think we're smart. You wanted strength but no thinking."

Jorry heaved a sigh and looked patient. "I wasn't recruiting for an academy, my friend. Were you the wisest man in the galaxy or the biggest fool, it made no difference to me as long as you were strong and could be trusted. At least in your case I judged correctly. I made my share of mistakes with the others. They were careless. Stupid. With a little luck, we could have beaten this planet. Next time, we will."

"Keoffo was watching," the Quespodon said.

Jorry breathed deeply and caught at his chest in sudden pain. "I don't care who was watching. Bring me more water, and leave me alone. Wait—bring me zaff leaves, too."

"You've had a lot, Jorry."

"I want more. My ribs hurt. Do as I order, Axxal, and do it quickly," Jorry commanded.

Axxal brought the powerful drug to his captain. Jorry folded one leaf into a compact wad, placed it in his mouth, and began to chew. Soon his eyes glazed and he lay back. Pain was gone now. Axxal set another carafe of water at the side of Jorry's bunk, and left.

When Jorry woke again and summoned him, Axxal found his captain looking and sounding more like his old self. He rose from his bunk with evident difficulty and pain he could not conceal, and yet his first order was for Axxal to remove the bandages.

"You need them, Jorry. You might have broken ribs," Axxal pointed out.

"I want them off. Get to work or I'll tear them off myself."

"But why, Jorry?"

"Because it pleases me."

"That's no reason."

"It's as good a reason as you're likely to get in this galaxy, my boy. Take it and cherish it."

As Axxal set about his work he mumbled, "You speak like Keoffo. 'It pleases me.' Just like Keoffo."

"And who in the blazing rings is Keoffo? I've heard you mumble his name a score of times. Is he some Quespodon god?"

"We have no gods. Keoffo is our Over-being."

"God or Over-being, call them what you like, Axxal, or don't call them at all. It means little to me." Jorry paused, then said with evident amusement, "So, I remind you of one of your Over-beings, do I?"

"Sometimes you make me think of Keoffo, but not often. Keoffo destroys. We call him the Trickster. He is the Spoiler of Plans . . . the Disrupter."

"It must be a great consolation to have something like that watching over you," Jorry said drily. "Do you believe in this Keoffo, Axxal?"

Axxal hesitated for a moment. He looked searchingly at Jorry, then he thrust out his thick forearms. "When I look at my skin, I think of the tale told of Keoffo: how he saw some races created for power, others for beauty, or wisdom, and then he created the Quespodons for a joke. No other race wears these markings—only the Quespo-

78

don. No other race is thought foolish and simple by all in the galaxy."

"Don't feel so sorry for yourself," Jorry said. "Your hide is scarcely mottled at all, and you can think as well as most men. You had the brains to get me aboard the *Seraph* and bind up my ribs. You even saved our weapons. The others may have laughed at you, but you're alive now and they aren't. Maybe you've outsmarted your trickster god this time."

Axxal shook his head. "Keoffo always triumphs."

"If you let him."

"I can do nothing. I try, Jorry, but there is no fairness in this galaxy, not for a Quespodon."

Jorry laughed aloud, wincing at the sudden stab of pain this brought about. He turned to Axxal and said, "Axxal, my boy, learn one thing from old Captain Jorry if you learn nothing more. If you expect fair treatment from this galaxy you ask for what never was and never will be, and you're a far bigger fool than the worst of your breed. The stars aren't your friends or mine. The galaxy isn't your mother and father. It's you against everything, Axxal. That's what it means to be alive. All of life is just a grand game, and the first rule is never to abide by the rules. They change at every move, and all the players are cheats. Perhaps we can't win—I'm not entirely sure of that—but we can put off losing for a long long time, and even when we've lost we can refuse to acknowledge it. It takes cleverness and skill to stay ahead, and a lot of k'Turalp'Pa tricks that others like to condemn because they're not clever or skillful enough to use them. You have to cheat with both hands just to keep up—if you want to come out of this life ahead, you'll have to cheat all the harder. Expect everyone—anyone—to treat you fairly and you'll be ground to a pulp. Now, stop whimpering and finish your work. I have a lot to do. We have to get off this murderous planet before it swallows us."

Axxal looked at his captain apprehensively. "I've already laid in a course. We've been spaceborne for twenty-six watches."

79

"You're full of surprises, Axxal. Where are we heading?"

"Xhanchos."

"Good enough. Did you pick Xhanchos for any special reason?"

"Oh, yes," Axxal replied eagerly. "I once heard you say that the Xhanchilion value gems very highly. They'll pay us the best price."

"The best price for what?" Jorry said sourly. "The treasure is buried under the citadel."

"We have the jewels Fimm pried from the door. I have mine, and I took Bral's and Dolul's and Fimm's from their bodies, and—" Axxal checked his tongue and began digging in his tunic for the proof of his words.

"Enough!" Jorry cried, laughing aloud until a pain in his ribs silenced him. "Axxal, I'm beginning to think that I should have put this entire undertaking in your hands. I need some time to think. Get me food and water and leave me alone."

Axxal followed his captain's instructions gladly. He, too, wanted time to be alone and to reflect on what had happened to them on this expedition. Axxal seldom thought of the past; indeed, he did his best to keep it from his mind, because it had been an unhappy time. But Jorry had revived old doubts and uncertainties in his mind. Jorry had reminded him, in ways that could not be denied, that he was at once a Quespodon and one unlike all others of his kind.

The Quespodons were known throughout the galaxy for two things: enormous strength and low intelligence. On every world, even their homeworld, they were the inferiors.

Quespodons served as draft animals for more advanced races, and as the butt of laughter for all who knew them. They were fit to labor hauling stone for the vanity of petty kings, or die battling in an arena for the fleeting amusement of weary aristocrats; they were worthy to carry other races' burdens, and live lives regulated by the more fortunate; but nowhere were Quespodons their own masters. Even on their homeworld of Dumabb-Paraxx, relays of otherworlders owned and managed the affairs of the planet and its people.

For most Quespodons, this was the accepted order of the galaxy. To rebel, even to question, was to risk the wrath of Keoffo, who had made things so for his own pleasure. But Axxal had moments of doubt. He still remembered the long-ago day when his father, hearing him speak fearfully of Keoffo, had said, "I sometimes wonder whether Keoffo made us for his own whim, or the otherworlders created Keoffo to make us what we are."

Axxal trembled at such words, for he knew that Keoffo would not let such speaking go unpunished. But when some time passed and nothing happened, he reconsidered, and at last summoned the courage to press his father for an explanation. His father counseled patience. Axxal waited, and the blow fell: His parents were carried off by Daltrescan slavers.

It was clearly retribution, and for a time Axxal was stricken with fear that the wrath of the Trickster might fall on him as well. But Keoffo, in his antic way, chose to be indulgent. He sent the *Seraph* to Axxal's world. Jorry took the orphaned Quespodon aboard as his orderly over the objections of some of the crew, and had treated him well ever since.

Axxal was loyal to his captain out of simple gratitude, but he could never bring himself to trust him fully. Jorry did not look upon people as *people,* but only as utensils for attaining his own ends. Now that the others were dead, Jorry did not even mention their names except to blame them for the failure of the expedition. He did not look upon them as lost comrades, but as tools that had broken or worn out. He cared nothing for them, and Axxal knew that he meant no more to Jorry than did anyone else. Jorry called him "son," and "good lad," but Axxal felt that under the proper circumstances, he would be expendable. The k'Turalp'Pa were a cold race, and as unpredictable and capricious as Keoffo himself. Even worse, in Axxal's mind, was the fact that the k'Turalp'Pa were closely associated with the Old Earth pioneers. The men of Old Earth had done little to endear themselves to their galactic neighbors in the days of first contact. The Quespodons had not been the worst treated, but they had their painful memories.

Axxal was the twelfth generation of his family to be born and raised off the homeworld, and he often wondered if this was what made him different. Other Quespodons were mottled with patches of blue and purple on their pale skin; Axxal's markings were scarcely distinguishable, his skin a nearly uniform rust color. And unlike other Quespodons, he could think and reason. If he could not, he and Jorry would now be buried beneath the citadel. Jorry himself had pointed that out.

But how, he asked himself, could such a thing be? His blood was pure Quespodon. No other race had purified the strain, because no other race would willingly mate with his. And yet he was different. Something had caused it, and he had to find out what, and why. It might be no more than a whim of the Trickster; he could not decide.

He often pondered this. Was Keoffo truly behind all that befell his people? Or had his father been correct to question the very existence of the Trickster? A people taught from birth that they were no more than the prank of an Over-being, created to amuse a mightier power that they could never fathom, forced to suffer or rejoice at his whim and marked for all the galaxy to see and scorn . . . such a people would come to believe their inferiority. By believing in it, they would make it true. So far, Keoffo had always triumphed. But perhaps, as Jorry said, only because the Quespodons had let him. Perhaps Keoffo himself—if he existed—could be tricked.

Axxal thought long and deeply on these things, and found no answers. He would not mention his troubles to Jorry, for fear of mockery, but during the long voyage to Xhanchos he attempted, indirectly, to learn what he could from the captain. Shipboard duties on a driveship were minimal, and Jorry was still convalescent; the two men had much time to talk.

"One mistake I regret more than any other," Jorry said at the end of a dull meal. "I should have hired on a bard, or a story-teller, or at least taught you to play chess, or quist, or sakooshe. The boredom is ruining my mind, Axxal."

"A few watches more and you'll be able to move around and get some exercise."

"I had all the exercise I want on Boroq-Thaddoi, thank you. I want no more until we reach Xhanchos, and then I'll take my exercise with a gorgeous green Gafaal lady. Have you ever seen a Gafaal courtesan, Axxal?"

"No. I've heard they're very beautiful."

"Oh, they are, my boy, they certainly are," Jorry said appreciatively. "Consorts to kings and emperors, that's what the Gafaal women are—though they do take kindly to starfarers."

"Do they really, Jorry?"

"Yes. And I venture to predict that they'll look with special kindness on a pair of starfarers who can buy half of Xhanchos with a single stone."

"Not for me," Axxal said. "Quespodons stay with their own women."

Jorry studied him for a time, then said, "Forgive my bluntness, Axxal, but it's always appeared to me that Quespodons are faithful to one another because they have no choice. You, on the other hand, have a choice. You're a wealthy man now, and besides, you don't look all that much like a Quespodon. You've got a good mind, too. Why not enjoy yourself while you can?"

"I am what I am, Jorry. I can't change it, even though I might be able to deceive some people."

"Still afraid of Keoffo, are you?"

"Sometimes I am," the Quespodon admitted. "And sometimes I think of the stories and can't help laughing. They are only fit for children."

"What story do your people tell of their origin?" Jorry asked.

"Long ago, when the First Over-being, the ruler of all the stars, was creating inhabitants for his worlds, he

83

gathered together all the good qualities people might possess," Axxal began. "And then, one by one, he chose a quality and made a new race to enjoy it. For courage, he made Skeggjatts; for pride, the Lixians; for cunning, the k'Turalp'Pa; speed, Malellans; agility, the Quiplids, and so on, for all the known races of the galaxy, except for the Quespodons. When he came to the end, only strength was left, and the ruler of stars chose to wait before creating his last race. He slept, and as he slept, the Trickster, Keoffo, came. He envied the ruler of stars and wanted a people all to himself, to bear the brunt of his jokes. He stole the last good quality and made the first Quespodons. But the ruler of stars awoke before Keoffo was finished. He saw what had happened, and he was enraged. In his anger, he struck Keoffo with his measuring rod—this is why Keoffo limps—and hurled him from the dwelling place of Over-beings. Keoffo, as he fell, flung away the Quespodons he had made to the world called Dumabb-Paraxx, the unfinished world. They fell far, and landed hard, and their bruises still appear on all their descendants."

"For a prankster, Keoffo seems a sour sort," Jorry observed. "I'd dislike living under his rule."

"This is only a story."

"So you say, Axxal. I think it's more than just a story to you, but that's your business, not mine. Tell me, do all Quespodons learn that story?"

"They do."

Jorry grunted thoughtfully, nodded, and was silent for a time. Then he said, "Let me take my turn and recite another creation story for you. This one comes from the Thorumbians. Collen sang it to me." Jorry took a drink of water, cleared his throat, sipped the water once again, propped his feet up on the mess table, and began a melodious chant.

"Maker took the dry reeds,
Watered them with saliva from his mouth,

Made the tall dry people,
Called them the Lixians.

Maker looked and looked again, and was not satisfied.
He took the round stones of the riverbed,
Dried them with the breath from his mouth,
Made the hard round people,
Called them the Quespodons."

"That isn't right, Jorry. That isn't how the Quespodons were made," Axxal interrupted.

"It doesn't matter. I don't believe your account of how the k'Turalp'Pa were made, but I didn't carry on about it. Just for that, I'm going to skip down to the end," Jorry said crossly.

"Maker looked at all that he had made,
Looked at all the people of all the worlds,
And with nothing was he satisfied.
Then he took the black soil from the high places,
Kneaded it in his strong hands,
Added the dark blood from his own veins,
Dried it in the sun,
Spoke to it in strong words,
And the black forms moved and spoke and worshiped
    Maker,
And Maker was satisfied.
Now he had the Thorumbians.
They were his people forever.
Now he was satisfied."

"Even though it's wrong about the Quespodons, that's a good story," Axxal admitted. They were silent for a time, then Axxal turned a puzzled look on Jorry and asked, "Why are there so many stories, all different? Why isn't there just one?"

"Because everyone's guessing."

"Don't always joke with me, Jorry."

"I'm not joking. I've been around this galaxy for a long

time, and I've never met a creature who really knows how it all began, and why. Nobody knows the truth, Axxal, that's the answer to your question. And if they did know, why would anyone tell?"

Axxal frowned in perplexity and responded, "Why not? Wouldn't it help everyone to know why we're all here?"

"You sound like one of the monastics on Urush Val-Zul. The fact is, we all know. Inside us, even if we don't admit it, we know. We're alive to get all we can and keep it for as long as we can. That's what life is about. Everyone out for everything he can get."

Axxal shook his head. "I don't think so, Jorry. That kind of thinking makes for a hard life."

"It *is* a hard life, my lad. A Quespodon ought to know that better than anyone."

"But it can be a good life. Sometimes people help each other."

"Not *my* people."

"What creation story do your people have, Jorry?"

"They never bothered to dream one up."

"But don't you wonder how you got here? And why?"

"What counts to us, Axxal, is that we're here. We can't change where we came from, so why concern ourselves with it? Never mind all this. You think about that Thorumbian story."

"Why?"

"Compare it with your own. You'll find some interesting differences."

"Anyone can find differences. The stories are of two very different races."

"Quite right. The Thorumbians are a proud people, while the Quespodons . . ." Jorry broke off and looked expectantly at Axxal, as if inviting him to complete the thought. When the Quespodon made no response, Jorry said, "Well, you think about it, Axxal. Let me know if you learn anything."

II.

Learning

In the long watches, Axxal thought much about Jorry's Thorumbian tale and the mocking invitation that followed it. The more he thought, the more confused he became, and often he called down bitter curses on whatever power had made his mind so different from his people's and caused him such unrest.

Other Quespodons could accept their lot. If they were not happy, at least they were untroubled by questions that had no answer. But such soothing acquiescence was no longer possible for Axxal. Without his seeking it, a door had been opened to him. He had chosen to take the first halting steps outside, and now there was no turning back. His problems became his daily companions, and though his only conclusion was that a curious mind is a bothersome and frustrating appendage for a Quespodon, he knew that he could not be happy if restored to a condition of mindless tranquility.

There was so much to be learned, and Jorry was the only one to whom he could turn for guidance. But as the *Seraph* drew ever nearer to Xhanchos, Axxal found it increasingly difficult to speak with him. Jorry's injuries had mended well, but the expedition to Boroq-Thaddoi had changed him. He kept to himself, and drank much Stepmann wine. His temper was short. He laughed less frequently and his laughter had a bitter ring to it. More often than not, it was directed at himself.

After a few unfortunate attempts to draw his captain into conversation, Axxal gave up and devoted his time to studying the workings of the *Seraph*. If he could not learn about himself, he reasoned, he would learn about the ship. His mind would not be idle.

There was much for Axxal and all his fellow inhabitants of that era to learn; but they had no living teachers. The driveships that bore them from system to system had all been built centuries before. They were products of a technology that collapsed forever when the humans of Old Earth, the greatest technicians in the history of the galaxy, had scattered throughout the stars like grains of sand flung into a hurricane. The ships endured, but the civilization that had produced them was forgotten, its records lost, scattered among a thousand worlds as fragments of myth and legend. The Wroblewski coils, the very heart of the lightspeed drive, worked on as efficiently as they had on their maiden voyages six centuries before, but the principle that underlay them was long forgotten. If a part broke or wore out—a rare occurrence—the crew or even the passengers, provided they could read, could replace it by following the ancient manuals. But the manuals did not explain purpose or function. The driveships were designed to carry fugitives by the millions from a festering planet; they were made literally foolproof. And needing no knowledge of their vessels' operations, the pioneers sought none.

In the great age of exodus, during the twenty-first and twenty-second centuries of the Galactic Standard Calendar, the factories of Old Earth turned out driveships in profusion. Enough were built, and in sufficient variety, to carry starfarers for centuries to come.

The first wave of pioneers settled where they landed, so shaken by the experience of deep-space travel that they drove all thought of it from their minds and rejected the history that had driven them to the stars. Their grandchildren, the second wave of voyagers, accepted the great ships as the figures in the ancient tales accepted flying carpets and winged steeds. The things moved, and took them to the fringes of the galaxy. They did not care to inquire how; they went.

So Axxal found himself in a position somewhat analogous to that of an Old Earth caveman placed in the cab of a nineteenth-century locomotive, or at the helm of a twenty-first-century space ferry. This immense and frightening construction moved; with some study, he could learn to control it; but for all he knew or could determine, it was propelled by spirits.

Axxal's mind was not as quick, nor as complicated, as Jorry's, but it was a methodical mind, a good tool for the slow and patient unraveling of a many-faceted but tangible problem. He applied himself to the workings of the *Seraph;* traced intricate circuits from source to destination; learned what they did, though he could not yet fathom how; even puzzled out what gave the *Seraph* a stable atmosphere and planetary gravity. With extreme difficulty, he deciphered the shifting points of light in the vision tank that formed the forward bulkhead, and grasped the rudiments of interstellar navigation. Heretofore, he had only been able to aim the *Seraph* at preprogramed destinations; now he saw that it was possible to choose his destination from any world on the charts.

These were exciting and frustrating days for Axxal. He had so very much to learn, and he did not know how to begin. But he persevered and found his efforts rewarded. Much still remained a mystery to him, but he did not allow the awareness of his ignorance to dampen his joy in new-found knowledge.

At the end of one watch, Jorry came upon Axxal on the bridge, where the orderly was studying the bright points of light in the depths of the vision tank. For a time, Jorry said nothing, and Axxal remained unaware of his presence. When Jorry spoke, Axxal started at the sound of a voice.

"So this is where you hide. What do you think you're looking at, a motion painting?" Jorry demanded.

"No. I'm trying to figure out how this works."

"Are you, now? And why would you suddenly be so interested in navigation? Do you have some plans that you're not telling me?"

"No, Jorry," Axxal said, stung by the accusation. "I only want to learn."

"That must be very frustrating for you, my boy. You can't learn anything by yourself, and I'm too busy to teach you."

Axxal's response was immediate and eager. "I can learn by myself, Jorry. I've figured out how the air stays pure even though the *Seraph* is sealed tight, and I think I understand the guidance system."

"You've had a good deal of time on your hands, haven't you? Is there nothing to keep you busy, that you can spend watch after watch poking your nose into the workings of the *Seraph?*" Jorry asked irritably.

"No, Jorry, that's just it—the ship cares for itself, and that's what got me interested. You were always busy, so I started looking more closely into the way the *Seraph* works."

Jorry listened impassively, then nodded, and admitted, "I never understood it myself, to be truthful, and never cared to. She's a good ship, and that's all I need to know, and I'll not have a Quespodon knowing more than I do about my own ship. Besides, I feel like some of that good Stepmann wine, and I'm tired of drinking it alone. Come along, my friend. You're invited to the captain's table. Consider yourself honored."

Axxal knew that he had no alternative; Jorry was to be obeyed. He would have preferred to continue his study of the vision tank, but he consoled himself with the recollection that Jorry always grew talkative when he drank, and was freer with his answers. The vision tank would remain; this was a chance to learn other things.

Jorry was indeed talkative, but not to Axxal's purposes. He wanted an attentive audience for a discourse on his own problems. He drank deeply, and grew more bitter as he proceeded.

"Six more watches to Xhanchos," he announced as he refilled their mugs for the third time. "What do you know about Xhanchos, my boy? Tell me what you've learned of the galaxy during all those watches spent in deep study."

"I didn't learn anything about Xhanchos. I only know it's a desert planet."

"A desert planet. Your knowledge is limited, but accurate. Xhanchos is a hot, dry, sandy, rocky, inhospitable world, but the city of Xhancholii is paradise. Or so I've been told, and shall continue to believe until I see otherwise for myself. One spot of beauty on an ugly desert world. A fine symbol of the whole stinking galaxy, I'd say. Ah, but that city . . . cool gardens, fountains, towers built to trap the high breezes . . . and Gafaal women to welcome us. To welcome weary old Captain Jorry, at any rate. Tell me, Axxal, what will you do with your share? You've had time enough to make plans."

Axxal frowned. After some thought, he said, "I don't know."

"You'll be wealthy. Has that occurred to you? I'm splitting everything right down the middle, half for you and half for me. That's after the captain's share, of course. We mustn't forget the captain's share. Fair enough for you?"

"Sure, Jorry. I trust you."

"You trust everyone. You'd do well to be less trusting when you're walking around the streets of Xhancholii with the price of a planet in your keeping. Tell me, what would you like to do?"

Axxal shook his head helplessly. He found it difficult to keep his thoughts in order. "I told you I don't know, Jorry. I never thought about that."

Jorry set his mug down and pointed at his orderly. "Now, there's your trouble, Axxal. You don't think about things. And that's a fine bit of irony for you, too, because old Captain Jorry's biggest problem is that he *does* think about things. We're both too trusting for our own good, but I think too much and you don't. Jorry thinks, and plans, and plots, and works everything out to the last detail . . . and he goes about it carefully, never rushing, patient as a man can be . . . and when he's all finished, what happens? When he's tracked down a legend that's been tantalizing starfarers for a galactic century and found a world that most of them will swear doesn't exist, and devised a way to breach a citadel that was made to keep out entire armies, what happens? What happens, Axxal?"

Somewhat muddled in his thinking by this time, Axxal said, "He comes out with a sackful of jewels. That's not so bad, is it, Jorry?"

Jorry filled his mug again. He pondered Axxal's words and nodded weightily. "No, it's not so bad. We were lucky, after all." He drank deeply, then went on, "But what's the use of thinking if it all comes down to luck? Why pick out a crew man by man when all you get is backstabbers and clumsy fools who can't dodge a boulder or fight off a stupid eyeless beast? Bral was the finest warrior I've ever seen, and he died for want of a little puff of air. You had the sense to raise your arm, but Bral . . . Rull-Lamat could have figured out . . . Even Jimm, poor little Jimm, got careless. . . ."

"But we got out alive, Jorry, and we didn't leave empty-handed. That's more than anyone's ever done before."

Jorry made no reply for a time. He scratched his neck, rubbed his forehead hard, and frowned. At last he slammed his mug down on the table top and said loudly, "I'm a k'Turalp'Pa. Plotting and planning is my whole life. In a universe without rules, without reason, I create order. For a brief moment, I govern the universe with my own mind."

"Nobody can do that, Jorry! Things never work out the way we plan!"

Jorry grinned sardonically. "Blame the universe for that, my boy. Not me or my people. We do our share. It's the universe that doesn't know its duties. I've spent most of a lifetime planning the assault on Boroq-Thaddoi, and I planned it to perfection, picked the crew myself . . . and it failed. What good is a handful of stones to me when I know I've failed? Axxal, I've lived a long and busy life under these stars. I've sold planets to gullible fools, taken driveships from under their owners' noses, fought my way out of three blackjacket ambushes. I've been king of a fine planet. The Windwalkers of Triffit II called me a god. And I've been a prisoner, too, in some of the grimmest dungeons in the galaxy. But I always held out hope of being the one who'd conquer Boroq-Thaddoi. One great feat to set me above all my people, and then I'd relax and do as I please. We're a long-lived race, Axxal, and I meant to spend my share of that long life savoring my accomplishments. All I have to savor now is my failure."

"How can you say you failed, Jorry? We're alive, we've got the *Seraph*, and we have the stones. That isn't failure," Axxal said earnestly.

"I didn't get it *all*, Axxal. For me, for any k'Turalp'Pa, that's failure."

"You did more than anyone else has ever done."

"I'm not competing with other people. No one else has ever done anything worth beating. I'm competing against myself, my own plans. I'm going back, and next time, I'll get it all. I know the way now." Jorry drained his mug, refilled it, then abruptly said, "Go away, Axxal. Go off somewhere and study the *Seraph*'s guts. I have plans to make. I'll tell you when it's time to begin landing procedure. Go!"

Axxal left at once, walking rather unsteadily. Between the wine and Jorry's behavior, he was badly confused.

The remaining watches passed, and the moment of transition arrived. The *Seraph* dropped below drivespeed. The stars reappeared and blazed on all the screens. The main viewer showed a cloudless world, bathed in gold, looming before them. Charts indicated one landing ring, deep in the desert. The *Seraph*'s scanners showed a second, newer one, just outside the walls of Xhancholii. It was on this ring that Jorry set the *Seraph* down.

III.

Monarch of Xhanchos

In the loose gray belted tunics of a free trader and his servant, Jorry and Axxal set out for the gate in the high wall that encircled Xhancholii. Night was falling. The city gleamed under three full moons and a sky thick with stars. Soft lantern glow shone at intervals atop the wall.

Concealed on his person Jorry bore one flawless jewel. The rest remained on the *Seraph,* which rose from the landing ring at their backs, secured against intrusion.

As they neared the gate, four men emerged and approached them on foot. Jorry disliked their looks. They were husky, dark-haired and pale-skinned, much resembling one another in features, and identically dressed in colorful uniforms. He had seen such men before, and he wondered at their appearance here.

"Are they Xhanchilion?" Axxal asked, confused. "They look more like your people."

"They're Skorat. I've heard that Xhanchilion kept slaves from other worlds, but these four don't walk like slaves. I think it's best if you know absolutely nothing from this point on, Axxal. I'll make up a story to explain our visit when the situation is clearer, but I don't want you talking to anyone, understand?"

Axxal nodded. The Skorats were within hearing distance by this time. Jorry raised his hand in peaceful greeting and hailed them. Their hands remained on their sword hilts and their grim expressions were unchanged. Jorry halted and hooked a thumb in his belt, ready—if the need arose—to go for his concealed blades. The Skorats, too, stopped in a line before them, and their leader addressed Jorry in the common tongue.

"State your name and business on Xhanchos."

"I'm Kian Jorry, free trader. This is my servant, Axxal. We come in peace, seeking trade."

"Are you slavers?"

"Do I look like a Daltrescan? Does that look like a slavers' hulk?" Jorry asked, jerking a thumb toward the *Seraph*.

"Answer questions, don't ask them," the Skorat responded.

"No, we're not slavers. As I said, we've come to trade."

"What goods do you carry? I see none."

"I'm willing and eager to discuss that with the proper authority, when you conduct me to him."

The Skorat thought on this answer for a time, then drew his comrades together to take counsel. Axxal edged closer to Jorry and said in a low voice, "Let's get off this planet. We can handle these four. They're no bigger than we are."

"We could take them, but we might not make it back to the *Seraph*." With a slight gesture of the head, Jorry indicated a dozen Skorats mounted on big desert haxopods waiting in the shadows of the gate. "Cheer up, Axxal. Skorats always talk boldly and then back down before someone who doesn't show fear of them."

Jorry's estimate proved true. He and Axxal were conducted through the city to the palace, and on the way Jorry observed much that made evident a change in the rule of Xhancholii. The streets were strangely empty. He had heard of this city as a busy, crowded place, but it now looked like the scene of a great plague, or the site of a disastrous battle. He saw not one male Xhanchilion, and very few females. Nowhere did he hear the high, chirping speech native to this civilization. All around them were otherworlders: Trulbans and Quespodons, Thorumbians, Agyari, Zotaron, men of Gilead and Skorat, burly Skeggjatts, and other races still unknown to him. The air was filled with the guttural sounds of the common language, peppered with the private oaths and expressions of every speaker's race. Jorry saw none of his own people, and this pleased him. No k'Turalp'Pa was to be found here because the k'Turalp'Pa were too clever to have been captured in the first place.

What had been a suspicion in Jorry's mind gradually became a certainty: somehow, the Xhanchilion had been overthrown and their former slaves had become masters of the city. The fact that some of the otherworlders were severely wounded, hobbling along on stumps, missing a limb or an eye, confirmed him in his opinion. Only under a new regime would cripples walk these streets. The Xhanchilion would have disposed of them.

Jorry turned to the Skorat who marched beside him and asked casually, "How long since you overthrew the Xhanchilion?"

The guard gave him a cold look. "Long enough, trader. Do you regret it? Would you rather be dealing with those flat-faced slavedrivers?"

"Not at all, my friend. I confess I'm relieved. I've heard of men who came here to trade and found themselves hauling stone out in the desert."

"And still you came here? You're a greedy one."

Jorry looked at him innocently. "Trade is like battle. The greater the risk, the higher the reward."

The Skorat turned that over in his mind, scowling, then announced, "You talk nonsense. Trade is not like battle."

Jorry shrugged. "Have it your way, friend."

At the palace they were informed that Gariv, monarch of Xhanchos, would receive them sometime before sunrise. Jorry agreed to wait, but demanded that they be fed at once. The palace officials blustered, but at last summoned two young Xhanchilion women to bring food and drink for Gariv's guests. As he dined, Jorry chatted with the servants, joked with the guards, and in bits and pieces extracted the story of what had taken place. It was as he had already guessed: The slaves had seized their camp in the desert and armed themselves. One night their army had burst upon the unsuspecting city. After a bloody, merciless, two-day battle, the city was theirs. And now, although they did not speak of it openly, tension was increasing among the victors.

Jorry observed that here in the palace, wearing the uniform of the guards, were only Skorats and Skeggjatts, men of warrior races. Apparently the others were already denied proximity to the throne. Jorry's heart warmed at the words he heard and the sights he saw. He had a comforting premonition that the situation could be manipulated to his benefit, once he had made himself fully acquainted with the facts.

It was late into the long Xhanchilion night before a guard came to Jorry to announce the monarch's readiness to see him. As Jorry and Axxal arose, the guard blocked the Quespodon's way with his sword.

"Your servant stays here," he said.

"I'd prefer to bring him with me," Jorry replied.

"The monarch of Xhanchos does not receive Quespodons."

Jorry saw nothing to be gained by disputing the new ruler's protocol. He instructed Axxal to wait, and entered the throne room alone.

The chamber was a large hexagon, high-roofed, decorated with tiles and wall designs in a gaudy barbaric pattern. In four of the six corners were guards, big fellows, Skeggjatts by the look of them, and in the center stood two thrones. On the higher and larger throne sat a man about Jorry's height but somewhat huskier in build. His coloring was much like Jorry's. He had the typical dark hair and beard of the Skorats, but much streaked with white. Despite this suggestion of age, he seemed to be in his prime. He wore with dignity the wide, bright baldric of office over his plain tunic. A simple crown rested on his head. Jorry glanced at him quickly and turned his eyes at once to a more agreeable sight.

Beside the Monarch of Xhanchos, on a smaller throne, sat a Gafaal woman of unparalleled beauty. A soft clinging robe of pure white accented her full figure and set off her emerald skin and dark red hair. Her hair, and the slim tentacles of her neck, were intertwined with a rope of gold to form a high crown. Jorry looked at her appreciatively, then bowed to each of the thrones in turn.

The monarch commanded, "Announce yourself."

"I'm Kian Jorry, Your Majesty. A free trader."

"I am Gariv of Skorat, Monarch of Xhanchos. This woman you find so much to your liking is Santrahaar, my consort."

Jorry bowed again, more deeply, to the woman. "I've seen much in my travels, but never on any world have I seen such a beauty as Santrahaar of Xhanchos. Truly, my eyes are dazzled."

"Well might they be. Did you come here to strain them, or to do business?" Gariv asked bluntly. "Where are you from, what do you offer, and what do you want?"

"My ancestry is Old Earth, Your Majesty, but I'm a free trader. My driveship is my true home. I've known no home but the *Seraph* since my early years."

"So you're Old Earth, are you? We of Skorat have Old Earth blood in our ancestry," Gariv said.

Jorry had learned long ago that flattery, however transparently insincere it might be, was a welcome sound to a newly minted king. It was useful, too, when a man was lying about himself and his intentions: It created a desire on the part of one's hearers to believe, and made the work at hand much easier. So he said, "I pride myself on the fact that I, a trader, share blood with the bravest warriors in our galaxy. May I presume to ask a question before going on?"

"I promise no answer, but you may ask."

"The present situation on Xhanchos confuses me, Your Majesty. Are the Xhanchilion truly defeated?"

Gariv smiled triumphantly. "Indeed they are, trader. We spared only enough of them to be our servants."

"Then all the slaves are free! Is that not so?"

"Many died in the battle. Some may yet die of their wounds. Of all who fought in the Free Army, we lost half."

Jorry looked up, sudden anguish in his eyes, and said

half-aloud, "To have come so close . . . Please, Your Majesty, tell me one thing more. Was there one among them named Jorry?"

Gariv shook his head. "None, trader. I knew every man's name, and none was named Jorry. Was he a kinsman?"

Jorry lowered his head and covered his eyes for a moment, then sighed and looked to Gariv and Santrahaar. "I came to Xhanchos on no ordinary business. I had a younger brother. I had hoped he'd join me on the *Seraph*, but he chose to become a healer. He left for Vigrid, in the Skeggjatt system, to study under the great surgeon Ingjald-Kolsson, but he never arrived. His driveship was taken by slavers. That was thirteen years ago, by the Galactic Calendar, and I've been seeking him all that time. I learned recently that a man of his description was brought to Xhanchos at about the time my brother disappeared. The other details tallied, so I came here, hoping to find him and buy his freedom."

Santrahaar spoke, and her voice was like sweet music. "Thirteen years of the Galactic Calendar are three Xhanchilion hranxluces. The people have told me that few otherworlders live more than a single hranxlux on the desert. Not even a Quespodon can survive much beyond that time. I give you sympathy, trader Jorry."

"I thank you, lady," Jorry answered in a breaking voice, "and I beg you to excuse me. After all this searching . . ."

"Many good men died hauling stone in that desert. If he had to die, it's a pity your brother couldn't have fallen battling for his freedom," Gariv interjected.

"True. Still . . ." Jorry sighed once again, then squared his shoulders and said, "I'd like to send a small remembrance to Your Majesty, if I may. My servant will be here tomorrow at nightfall with six decanters of the finest Stepmann wine. And for the Lady Santrahaar . . ." He reached into his tunic and drew out the jewel he had taken from the *Seraph*. It lit the throne room with a sudden blaze of inner fire, and as he turned it in his fingers, the glow flashed and shimmered on the brightly bedizened walls. He stepped forward and placed the jewel in Santrahaar's outstretched hands. She took it eagerly and laughed a girlish, innocent laugh of pure joy as she raised it before her eyes. "Thank you, Jorry. It's the finest stone I've ever seen. It's magnificent."

"Don't send your servant with the wine, trader," said Gariv. "Bring it yourself, and dine with us. There may yet be business for you on Xhanchos."

"With pleasure, Your Majesty. At nightfall, then?"

Gariv nodded agreeably.

"I thank you again, Jorry," Santrahaar said. "And I will wear your gift when we dine."

Jorry bowed respectfully and left the throne room quite pleased with the way things had gone so far. That gesture with the jewel had been a wise move: Impulsive generosity had a great effect on barbarians. Gariv was a typical Skorat—so swollen with his own self-importance that he could not imagine anyone's snatching a prize from his hands.

Xhanchos was not much of a world, really. But it was a paradise compared to Boroq-Thaddoi, and the company of Santrahaar would make it bearable for some time. And there were those pyramids standing out in the desert. Certainly they'd be worth investigating. It could make for a pleasant holiday, and a good place to plan for his return to Boroq-Thaddoi.

"Something's up, Jorry," Axxal greeted him. "I listened to the guards talking, and it sounds as though there's trouble ahead."

"I sense that myself," Jorry said. "We'll take a room nearby. While I'm dealing with Gariv, you can find out what's happening outside the palace. Let's hurry. It will be sunrise very soon, and the days on Xhanchos are too warm for my blood."

IV.

An Encounter

Axxal awoke at the midpoint of the long Xhanchilion day. Outside, the sun blazed down from an empty sky to raise the temperature of half of Xhanchos beyond human tolerance; but Axxal's sleeping chamber was dim and cool and comfortable. He lay half-awake for a time, mulling over the confused and disturbing situation that seemed to be developing on this world, and then, unable to sleep, he rose and dressed.

Jorry still slept, as a quick check of his chamber disclosed. He had stayed up well past sunrise, drinking the sour local vintage with others at the inn, chatting and joking and telling stories, and all the while drawing out of them everything they knew about the state of affairs. Axxal recalled his commission of the night before: He was to learn all he could of the local situation. He decided to begin by exploring Xhancholii now, on his own, before Jorry awoke. He breakfasted on a couple of the sweet blue-skinned fruits that lay in a dish in the main room, and then set out.

On the great desert that covered much of Xhanchos, nothing moved by day. All travel and all work were done by night, under the soft light of one or more of the seven moons. But in the city of Xhancholii, arcades and covered streets screened out the withering sun. Wind scoops atop the buildings trapped the high breezes to channel them down the shaded streets and over the clear fountains that danced at every crossing. Here, the daytime hours were bearable, even pleasurable. Among the rulers, the custom of conducting all important business and affairs of state by night still prevailed; but many of the former slaves associated sleep by day and work by night with their servitude. Thus, when Axxal left the inn, he found some parts of Xhancholii not much emptier than they had been by night.

The quarter of the city that held the palace and the official buildings was laid out in neat straight avenues, with wide arcades on either side of an open central passage; no crowds here. Beyond this area, conditions changed. Streets were narrow, winding, and uneven. Fountains were fewer, and many he saw were mere trickles. Often the water was dirty and stank. Palace uniforms were nowhere in evidence, nor were the Skorats and Skeggjatts who strutted in them elsewhere.

Axxal walked now among the women and children of the vanquished Xhanchilion, and the less-favored of the victors. Here were his own people, squat Quespodons with deeply mottled skin. Tall black Thorumbians, slender Agyari, fair-haired Trulbans, and other breeds Axxal had never seen before filled these cramped and dirty byways.

He walked on, studying everything, stopping here and there to refresh himself and make seemingly idle inquiries of those he met, until he came to a group of a dozen or more gathered at a crossway. A voice came from their midst. The voice was strong and clear, and Axxal heard every word. The language was the common tongue of the spaceways, but the intonation was unmistakably Quespodon. Axxal could not see the speaker. He stopped on the edge of the little crowd to listen.

"And you, Dabuxx—I saw your brother cut down on the steps of the temple when he took a blow meant for Gariv. Your brother gave his life for the arrogant Skorat, and now that Gariv is monarch of Xhanchos you're not even allowed in his presence," the voice said. "How do you like that, Dabuxx? Come, speak up, tell us how you feel about it."

A Quespodon near the front of the crowd answered, "I

don't want to go near the palace, Vaxxt. What would a Quespodon do at the palace, anyway?"

Some hesitant laughter followed this question, but the first speaker replied in a cold ironic voice that held no mirth. "You might run errands for our new masters, the Skorats and Skeggjatts who wear Gariv's colors. They might think you fit for such work. We should have known what they were planning from the very start, from the time Gariv organized the assault on Xhancholii. It was all clear then, if we hadn't been so gullible . . . if we'd had the sense to question."

"What did he do, Vaxxt?" a puzzled voice inquired.

"Have you forgotten the plan of attack? Gariv and all his Skorat kin, with their Skeggjatt lackeys, were the ones who rode against the gates. They were armed, every one, with the weapons we took from the camp. They were all mounted, and they had surprise on their side. But what of us? On foot we stormed an awakened city ready and waiting for us, and our only weapons were those we could seize. We were butchered, just as Gariv planned."

"But Gariv won us our freedom!"

Vaxxt's voice was contemptuous. "He freed us so we could die winning a world for himself and his followers. And I tell you now, those of us who survived the assault will soon—" He stopped abruptly at the sight of Axxal, who had pushed forward to see this speaker for himself.

Axxal was as surprised as Vaxxt at their first sight of each other: They looked enough alike to be brothers. Each had the chunky, heavily muscled build of their people, and both were hairless, but their markings were faint, their skins an identical rust color. In the glance that passed between them, recognition was instantaneous.

"Here's a stranger to our city," Vaxxt said warily. "You come in the dress of a free trader—what would you trade with the likes of us?"

A flurry of laughter quickly die, and Axxal said, "My employer does the trading."

"He's a generous employer, to do the work while you wander about listening to people talk."

103

"There's no work for either of us yet. My employer meets at nightfall with your King Gariv, and perhaps when—"

"Gariv is no king of ours, trader," Vaxxt broke in.

"Be careful, Vaxxt," a big Quespodon warned. "Your words might be passed on. We don't know who this fellow is."

Axxal replied angrily, "I told you who I am. I'm no spy, to listen to my own people speak their minds and run to tell their words to otherworlders."

Vaxxt's response was placating, his tone friendly. "We make no accusation. We merely try to be cautious. If you have the time, trader, I'd gladly speak further with you."

It was a good opportunity to learn more, and Axxal did not hesitate. The other dismissed the crowd with a final admonition: "Remember what I say, brothers. Gariv has plans for us, and if we make no plans of our own, we'll soon regret it. Think on this."

Only when Vaxxt started off did Axxal realize that he was a cripple. He tucked a single crutch under his arm and hobbled swiftly down the narrow passage, Axxal on one side and the big Quespodon on the other, brushing the walls as they passed. No word was spoken until Axxal and Vaxxt were seated in a dark corner of a nearby inn. The third Quespodon stood watch at the entry, out of earshot.

Vaxxt was direct. Axxal had scarcely told him his name when Vaxxt gestured impatiently and demanded, "How long have your forebears lived away from Dumabb-Paraxx? How many generations?"

"Eleven. I'm the twelfth."

"And they've always bred true? No marriage with otherworlders?"

Axxal laughed. "Have you found otherworlders so anxious to marry Quespodons? It wasn't so on our world. My blood is unmixed."

"I thought as much. I'm the eleventh generation since we left the homeworld, and I'm pure Quespodon. Now—"

look at us, Axxal. Do you see how we differ from all the others?"

"The markings . . . They're almost invisible."

Vaxxt nodded impatiently. "That's obvious. But what else? Haven't you noticed how different we are from our brothers on Dumabb-Paraxx?"

"I've met so few of them . . . but the ones I've seen all seem to me to be . . ."

"Go ahead, Axxal, say it," Vaxxt prodded him.

"They seem to be as foolish and brutal as all Quespodons are said to be. They don't *think*."

"True, they don't. But we do," Vaxxt said triumphantly. "You've found that, haven't you?"

"Yes. Yes, I have. There have been times . . . I understood things, figured out things that no Quespodon should have grasped. The gravity system on the *Seraph* . . . the way out of the citadel . . ."

"And at first, it troubled you, even frightened you. Like me, you were told by everyone you ever met that you're a fool sprung from a race of fools. But you're not, Axxal, and neither am I."

Axxal gestured helplessly. He wanted to run away before Vaxxt could say things even more troubling, and yet he ached to hear more. This was a thing he had long suspected. He felt a surge of joy, and sudden strength, and at the same instant, even as Vaxxt had said, he feared what was to come. He had been set apart. "Why *us?*"

"It has something to do with the homeworld, I'm certain of that much. The longer we're away from that pesthole, completely out of contact, the clearer our minds become. That's why there's now an emigration quota: the otherworlders don't want to lose their supply of strong, stupid workers. And it's why the gang of otherworlders who own everything on Dumabb-Paraxx are relieved at regular intervals: if they stayed, they'd be infected just as our ancestors were, long ago."

"If that's so, how did the first few Quespodons—your ancestors and mine—how did they get off the homeworld?"

"Maybe the Old Earthers took them along as replacements. Or as interesting pets. We'll never know, Axxal. They left no records for us. And then came the quota."

Axxal remembered old stories. "My father spoke of the quota. I remember his words."

"What was he like? Was he as intelligent as the otherworlders around him?"

"He was. Vaxxt. He told me the old legends—tales of the Trickster—and he said that he thought Keoffo might have been invented by otherworlders, just to keep us subservient."

"He was a wise man, Axxal."

"I couldn't make myself believe him then, although his words troubled me. Soon after he said that, Daltrescans carried him off. For a long time I feared that Keoffo had taken revenge on him for his words. Now I see . . ." Suddenly, pleadingly, he repeated his question. "But why us, Vaxxt? Why you and I, and no others?"

"Two reasons, Axxal, as far as I can tell: We're long away from the homeworld, and our blood is pure Quespodon. When I was brought here, I first met Quespodons from outside my own colony, and it was a shock to me. There were thirteen others in my work crew: eleven from the homeworld and two from a colony on Tilcha, where they had intermarried with planetaries over the generations. And every one of them was as brutal and ignorant and hideously blotched as all the tales of space made Quespodons out to be. The more of them I met, the more convinced I became that I was a freak of some kind."

"I sometimes thought the same thing," Axxal confessed.

"But I knew that the people of my colony were like *me*, not like these others. We couldn't all be freaks. And now that I've seen you, from another colony, I'm convinced. There may be more like us in the galaxy—those who escaped in the early days, before the quota, and never married otherworlders." Vaxxt leaned forward and said in slow words underscored by the intensity of his voice, "Axxal, the Quespodons are not the hopeless fools of the galaxy. They're the match of any race, given the chance."

Vaxxt spoke with eloquence and deep conviction. But had he stumbled over every word, Axxal would still have accepted all he said. These words made his heart beat faster. The unknown that he had sought from Jorry and the *Seraph* had been awaiting him on Xhanchos. "How do we give them the chance, Vaxxt?" he asked.

V.

A Future For Xhanchos

Jorry pressed a Xhanchilion youth into service to carry his gift of wine from the *Seraph* to the palace, but he conveyed it past the outer gates himself. To his surprise, he was conducted to no spacious dining hall but once again to the throne room, where he found a long table laid with bright napery and set with platters on which were heaped ripe fruits. Two stewards took the wine, and a third servant showed him to his place, where he awaited the entrance of the other diners.

Jorry's recent fortunes had not been at the zenith; but in the course of a long starfaring life he had seen, and twice ruled in, palaces to which the royal palace of Xhancholii was little better than an antechamber. Events and setting confirmed his impression of Gariv. Like every Skorat, the man was in his soul a barbarian. Accustomed to dwelling in a dirty fortress or a dusty tent, to dining on stringy rations made palatable by liberal drafts of coarse wine, he no doubt considered this gaudy chamber a scene of considerable splendor, proof in itself that the occupant was a king. Jorry came close to pitying him—but not too close. Whatever his limitations, Gariv ruled Xhanchos and had a force of tested warriors to uphold his power. He had Santrahaar for his consort. He was the host and Jorry the guest, he the master and Jorry the suppliant. But this state of affairs would not endure. Jorry was already weaving plans.

He rose and bowed respectfully as Gariv entered with Santrahaar at his side. The jewel Jorry had given her at their first meeting shone in her hair. In a revealing gown of brilliant red, she was more beautiful than ever, and he grew impatient to have her as his own. He remained standing until the royal couple had been seated and Gariv gestured him to his place.

"There'll be no others joining us. First we'll dine, trader, and then you and I will talk business," Gariv said.

"As Your Majesty wishes," Jorry said respectfully.

"Before we begin, I have a present for you. You're not the only one who knows how to give gifts." Gariv clapped his hands smartly and a pair of Xhanchilion came forward bearing a richly decorated haxopod saddle and riding harness. Jorry was a man who preferred to travel on his own two feet when he was not on the deck of a driveship, but he appreciated good workmanship. His thanks to Gariv were genuine. When the servants had removed the gifts, Santrahaar spoke.

"I, too, have something for our guest," she said, extending her hand and letting a pendant drop through her fingers to dangle from a slender chain. "Come to me, Kian Jorry, and I'll see that you wear it properly."

She drew Jorry closer and placed the pendant around his neck, arranging the chain so that the exquisitely worked piece of Xhanchilion bluestone caught in his tunic—a rich and colorful one, for this occasion—and hung fixed over his heart.

"Wear the bluestone over your heart, Kian Jorry, and you'll always win the love you most desire. This is an old belief of the Gafaal."

He smiled and looked into her eyes. "The love I most desire will be hard to win. A powerful man already claims her for himself."

"Powerful men are often disappointed." She smiled back. "Women have minds of their own. Even we of the Gafaal have been known to choose for ourselves."

"Some things are more than a lonely starfarer dares to hope for, my lady."

"Trust to the bluestone," she said softly.

"We've had enough talking and gift-giving," Gariv said with some impatience. "Now we dine."

Jorry found the meal surprisingly good, but he had difficulty suppressing his amusement at the musicians Gariv brought in to entertain them. Their ineptitude was without bounds. Gariv himself showed his displeasure by throwing a bowl of thick stewed fruits at them after they had twice mangled the ending of a simple Skeggjatt deed-song. Jorry and Santrahaar exchanged covert smiles as the trio of musicians fled Gariv's wrath, and the Monarch of Xhanchos turned to them in chagrin.

"Good feasting calls for good music, and there's not a musician on this planet worth the effort it takes to kick him. I brought a good one out of the camp—gave him the name of my old bard and anthem-maker, Alladale. Do you know of him?"

"The name is unfamiliar to me, Your Majesty."

"Then you've heard little, for all your traveling. He was the best in the galaxy, Alladale was. The *first* one, I mean, the real one. Not the clean-handed weeper I plucked from his chains and allowed to ride in the vanguard with my picked men. I'm well rid of him, even though he played to my liking."

"Did he fall in battle?" Jorry asked.

"He had no taste for it, this one. He made us a fine anthem, and when he saw the blood that ran in the streets, he wept over his own words and tried to tell me we'd gone too far. A coward, for all his word-skill. He's hiding somewhere now, he and his Xhanchilion woman." Gariv glowered, drank, and began, "Probably plotting . . ." He stopped himself, turned to Santrahaar, and commanded, "Leave us. I have matters of importance to discuss with the trader."

She rose, with a murmured "As Gariv wishes." She was a Gafaal, a trained courtesan, habituated to a display of complaisance. What feelings lay behind that mask of flawless beauty were her own secret, but for an instant, something flared in her eyes unnoticed by the Monarch of Xhanchos, and Jorry read it as loathing. It pleased him to see this. He knew that she had been bred for a better man than Gariv, and when she turned to bid her guest the ceremonial farewell, her hurried whisper told him all he wished to know. The bluestone had begun to work for him.

"She's decorative, but I don't trust her," Gariv said when Santrahaar was gone. "A prize of battle, that's all she is to me."

"A very lovely prize," Jorry said.

"Befitting me, trader," Gariv snapped. "I organized the escape. I led an army of slaves, two thousand of them, mostly unarmed rabble, against a walled city held by a force three times our number, and I overthrew an ancient dynasty. I deserve the most beautiful woman on the planet, and everything else that comes to me. You may look at her as much as you like, but never forget who won her, and who owns her."

"Never, Your Majesty," Jorry answered humbly. He found Gariv's chest-thumping a source of considerable amusement, but his time for open laughter had not yet come.

"Santrahaar is good enough for me while I'm on Xhanchos. But I have as fine a woman awaiting me on Skorat, when I choose to return." He took a small motion painting from around his neck and thrust it before Jorry. "Nikkolope, Queen of the city of Thak. My wife and regent. As good as a Gafaal woman, don't you think?"

Jorry was forced to agree. No race in the galaxy could compete with the Gafaal for sheer sensual beauty, but Nikkolope was a truly lovely woman with an inborn magnificence that lent radiance to her perfect features. Studying the lifelike image closely, Jorry concluded that Gariv's bluster had been of little use on Skorat. This was a woman too strong to be ruled by any man, though she would grace any ruler's side. The sight of Nikkolope, added to the memory of Santrahaar, piqued Jorry's sense of fitness: For the like of Gariv to have wedded one and taken the other as his consort was simply intolerable, and he felt personally obliged to remedy this situation at his earliest opportunity. For the present, however, he played his role of humble trader.

"I envy Your Majesty's good fortune. How long is it since you parted from Queen Nikkolope?"

"I left to join the Expedition. A good long time, but she waits," Gariv said confidently as he retrieved the painting.

"That's long for a ruler to be absent," Jorry observed.

"Nikkolope will wait. I won the right to seek her hand in fair combat," Gariv said. He pulled open his tunic to reveal a jagged scar. "See that? I got that fighting for her. I had to defeat nine others to prove myself."

Instinctively, Jorry touched his fingertips to his own chest. He, too, bore a scar, from a long-ago clash with the blackjackets. Gariv glared at him, and Jorry dropped his hand and asked politely, "Is that the usual method of courtship on Skorat?"

"If the lady wishes a warrior for a husband."

Jorry looked very much impressed. "You're a vigorous people. The custom on my world is simply to ask the lady." With a dry laugh, he added, "We get our scars after marriage."

Gariv saw no humor in the remark, but went on, as if Jorry had not spoken, "She rules the city of Thak in my name. Not a man on Skorat would dare to question her command."

Jorry nodded profound agreement. It occurred to him that Gariv's confidence might be ill-founded. The males of Skorat might well be as subservient as he claimed, but not for fear of a long-absent Gariv. From the look of her, Nikkolope would command obedience in her own right.

"It's not Skorat that concerns me now, trader. I'm thinking of the future here on Xhanchos," Gariv went on.

"Things seem to be well under control."

"It's too quiet. All the scum of the galaxy are gathered in the bowels of Xhancholii, and yet we see and hear nothing of them."

Jorry assumed a puzzled expression. "But surely Your Majesty doesn't want open unrest . . . ?"

"I'd prefer it to unnatural silence. Quespodons are stupid. They can easily be manipulated by a clever man. Al-

112

ladale might be hiding among them, stirring them up against me, though I doubt he has the stomach to lead an insurrection. And I wonder about Anders, the healer. He's a Skeggjatt, a warrior, and these mottled halfwits adore him. He saved scores of them after the assault, when it would have been simpler to let them die."

"Healers are like that," Jorry said with a sigh.

"Healers should do as their leader commands," Gariv said angrily. Suddenly he shot a suspicious glance at Jorry and said, "You brought a Quespodon servant, didn't you?"

"I did. I see to it that he behaves himself."

"Keep a close rein on him. The Quespodons here are up to something, I'm sure of it." Gariv laughed sharply, unpleasantly, and went on, "Not that they can plan much of anything, but with a capable leader . . ."

Jorry thought fleetingly of Axxal. He had been gone for the entire day, and had not yet returned when Jorry left for the palace; probably digging up information, as he had been directed to do. Axxal was fairly intelligent—indeed, impressively bright, for a Quespodon—but the thought of him as a leader was absurd, even as a leader among his own kind. The lad had curiosity and a certain slow, plodding aptitude for simple mechanics, true. But to devise long-range plans, to make decisions, to grasp and evaluate new facts instantaneously . . . no, these abilities were beyond him, beyond any Quespodon. Their race bred no leaders.

"My servant will do no leading, I'm sure of that," Jorry said, smiling.

"Someone may. They're ripe to be led." Gariv emptied his goblet, made a sign to Jorry to finish his, and ordered another decanter of Stepmann wine to be brought in. "The truth is, trader, I'd like them to rise against me." He gestured around at his guards and went on, "I've got a good force of fighting men, all loyal to me. They're the nucleus of a warrior class. We'll need servants, and the crushing of an uprising would justify any measures I choose to take against the rebels, and rid me of their leaders. That would leave only the rabble, to serve us without murmuring."

"Logical," Jorry observed.

"I've heard that there's talk among the Quespodons and their friends of forming a commonwealth."

"A commonwealth?" Jorry repeated uncertainly.

"An idiotic system in which leadership is placed in the hands of those who were born to be led," Gariv said heatedly. "In a commonwealth, servants are the equals of their masters."

"Madness, indeed," Jorry said, shaking his head.

"I see the future of Xhanchos clearly, trader. My men will take Gafaal as mates and create a race of aristocrats. The lesser breeds can have the Xhanchilion females, and provide us our servants and workers. All will have their proper place and duties. All will be happy."

"An eminently reasonable plan, Your Majesty," Jorry said, straight-faced. "Have you informed them yet?"

"No. They still think of themselves as free. They even fancy themselves warriors, because they were able to conquer a city once the Skorats and Skeggjatts in the vanguard had slain the defenders. But I've taken the first step."

"What's that?"

"A Daltrescan slaver is due to arrive at the end of the present moon cycle. The Quespodons counted on seizing it to take them home. That would leave us without servants and I can't permit such a thing. I've announced that the ship is not arriving, that no further ships will land on Xhanchos for a long time."

Jorry perceived the drift of Gariv's thought, but pretended ignorance. "How can you keep the ship from landing?"

"You'll do that for me, trader."

"I? How?" Jorry asked innocently.

"Simply keep your ship where it is. There's only one landing ring by the city, and I doubt that the Daltrescans' ships carry anyone capable of manual landings. When they find the ring occupied, they'll leave. I'll have the rabble here for good, and once they realize that there's no escape from Xhanchos, they'll soon come around to my view."

"What if the slavers return?"

"By the time they come back, if they do, everything will be under control. I'll send you to Skorat for colonists, and return home as ruler of two worlds."

"Brilliant, Your Majesty!" Jorry exclaimed. He paused, then cautiously asked, "But what would you have done if the *Seraph* had never come to Xhanchos?"

"I'd have been forced to strike down the Quespodons and the rest of the riffraff as soon as the Daltrescans had been overcome. It might have cost me good warriors, and I'm glad I can avoid it."

Jorry made a great show of marveling at Gariv's wisdom and judgment, and Gariv drank in his praise as readily as he downed the Stepmann wine. As the night wore on, the Monarch of Xhanchos promised ever more lavish rewards to the obliging free trader who had arrived so opportunely. When the last decanter of wine lay empty, Jorry was assured of a position at his ruler's right hand.

Jorry left the palace shortly before dawn. Gariv had stumbled to his chamber, where he now slept soundly, guarded by two loyal Skorats. He would sleep for a good long time, Jorry was sure of that.

So much the better, he thought. It gave him time to rest, to change, and to arrive refreshed for his midday rendezvous in another part of the castle. Things were going well.

VI.

Axxal Tells a New Tale

The room was crowded with Quespodons eager to hear the words of the cripple and the free trader. For many nights now, these two had spoken to groups of former slaves. This night, they spoke to an audience comprised solely of Quespodons.

Axxal had rehearsed his speech carefully and practiced every gesture; still, his husky frame trembled as he stepped before the silent crowd. But when he began to speak, the intensity of his message swept away all fear. His voice was firm and strong.

"I've visited far worlds and seen strange things," he began. "I could tell you many a tale of wonder. But I don't come here as a bard, to entertain you. Tonight I speak to you as a brother and bring you news that affects us all.

"In my travels I've met otherworlders of all breeds. Some of them have been good to me. When you were in the work camps, you, too, came to know otherworlders of good will. Alladale, the anthem-maker, sang songs to celebrate Quespodon courage, and the healer Anders saved many Quespodon lives after the battle. These otherworlders were good men and friends to the Quespodon. My partner in the trading venture that brought me to Xhanchos is an otherworlder, and he is a friend. This is how it should be between all the people of the galaxy.

"But it is not always this way, my brothers. Too often, otherworlders have caused us suffering. Think of yourselves. Daltrescans stole you from your homes, Xhanchilion enslaved you, and now Skorats and Skeggjatts, led by Gariv, plan to betray you. You look to doubt me, but I

116

can prove my words: Gariv has said that the Daltrescan ship will never return to Xhanchos. This is a lie!"

His words caused a stir. He let the assembled Quespodons express their surprise and excitement for a time, then raised his hands for order and cried, "Yes, Gariv has lied! He knows the slavers' driveship will arrive soon, but he plans to use it not to take us home to our own worlds. He means to bring more of his people here. They'll build a new kingdom on Xhanchos, and we will be their servants forever. But this we will not permit!"

"What can we do? How can we stop Gariv?" came the cries.

"Vaxxt knows what to do, and he will tell you. But I have more to say of otherworlders' treachery. Will you hear me out?" They roared their affirmation, and Axxal went on, "Then let me tell you of Keoffo, the Trickster. The story I tell is the true one, kept from you by deceitful otherworlders, the children of Old Earth, who lied to our forefathers in order to make them believe themselves mean and unworthy and fit only to serve the rest of the galaxy."

"Speak carefully when you speak of the Trickster! Even on Xhanchos, his power is great," someone called from the audience.

"The only tricksters we need fear from now on are the otherworlders who pretend to be our friends and then betray us. Keoffo died when the stars began to move. I don't fear him, brothers, I laugh at him!"

This was too bold a statement for some of those in the audience, and Axxal had to wait some time for order. When they were silent once again, he stepped forward and said, "Now hear the true story of Keoffo and the making of our people."

In a low voice that held their absolute attention, he began, "Long ago, when the stars were new and the worlds were empty, the ruler of stars decided to create one perfect race. He gathered together all the good qualities of body and mind, and assembled them around one perfect man and one perfect woman. They were to be the parents of all. But before he awoke them to life, he set out to visit all the worlds and choose the finest one for his people.

"While he was gone, Keoffo, his servant—a clumsy, stupid, evil servant he was, too, always undoing the good his master intended—this Keoffo chanced upon the perfect couple where they lay sleeping. He grew envious when he saw others so gifted and beautiful and well-formed, and his envy made him daring.

"With great care and caution—for he was a cowardly, sneaking rogue—he slipped up to them. He saw all the gifts and good qualities that lay around them. The ruler of stars was far away. Keoffo grew bold. He snatched away one of their gifts, their wisdom, and hurled it out into the darkness. When the ruler of stars did not return, Keoffo did the same thing once again, with their beauty. One by one he stole all their gifts, until only one was left out of all their creator had intended.

"And then the ruler of stars returned. He had found a perfect world for his people. He gave a command, and set the stars in motion, and then he turned to reach for the perfect man and woman. When he saw that their gifts were gone, he wept, and where his tears fell on their bodies, the skin turned blue and purple. He picked them up gently, lovingly, as a father lifts a sick child, and instead of putting them on the beautiful world he had picked for them, he placed them near him on Dumabb-Paraxx, the world of unfinished things. Then he sought out Keoffo."

"What of Keoffo? What did he do to Keoffo?" they cried.

"With his own hands, the ruler of stars broke him to pieces and scattered the fragments throughout the universe. Even now, this very moment, the pieces are still falling."

"Is this the true tale? Is it so?" voices asked.

"This is the truth, brothers," Axxal assured them. "The Quespodons are not the dregs of creation, the leavings of the ruler of stars, the handiwork of Keoffo. That was the lie of the Old Earthers who came to our world to make us a race of beasts like themselves. We were the first. We were the best. Our gifts were stolen from us, and we must regain them."

"How? How can we do this?" came from all sides.

"We must seek them among the stars and someday return to that perfect world meant for us. Some of us have already begun to win back the old gifts. One day all will have the chance. It will be hard, and it will take a long, long time, but we must begin now, here on Xhanchos."

Vaxxt's voice rang out over the murmurs of the crowd, silencing them instantly. "You've heard Axxal, and you know he speaks the truth. Quespodons were not born to serve, and those who say this, lie!"

"Why would the Old Earthers lie to us?" one Quespodon asked, rising to his feet. "When they came to Dumabb-Paraxx, they had driveships, great machines, tools for healing . . . things we could not even imagine. They were civilized."

"You call them civilized," Vaxxt said scornfully. "The Old Earthers fled a world they had bathed in blood and covered with foulness. For fifty galactic centuries they had devoted all their efforts—all their civilization, as you call it—to murder and destruction. Could such a race ever tell the truth?"

"But their accomplishments, Vaxxt . . . even if they lied to our forefathers, they had great skill, great achievements."

"So all people thought, at first," Vaxxt admitted. "But if you would speak of great accomplishments, speak of the ones you know best: the ruins on the homeworld."

Vaxxt's mention of the colossal fragments that stood on Dumabb-Paraxx brought a stunned silence to the gathering. No one had even a remote idea of who had made them, and the common solution to the mystery was to attribute them to the legendary First Travelers who had crossed the galaxy when the stars were young, begun these monumental works, and then departed to leave them unfinished. But Vaxxt had thought of a new answer: They might be the work of ancient Quespodons, a people

119

of great attainments reduced by some cataclysm of man or nature to their present state. The ruins that dotted the surface of their homeworld had long been a source of abasement to the Quespodons: proof of the glory of a vanished race, testimony to their own littleness. Their presence had made easier the task of those who would convince the Quespodons of their unworthiness. But Vaxxt had realized that they could be turned to the opposite purpose. They could serve as inspiration for a worn and weary race to raise itself to long-forgotten heights, and beyond, to a new greatness.

Vaxxt let the silence hang in the air of the room for a time, then said softly, "Ah, so you're thinking of them, are you? Picturing those broken towers and the shattered domes that once could have held all Xhancholii? Did the Old Earthers build *those,* brothers?"

"No. They couldn't have done that," his questioner admitted, and another cried, "It's said that the first Old Earthers were amazed at the sight of them!" Others shouted their agreement.

Vaxxt's voice filled the room. "Before Earthmen knew how to place one stone upon another, our ancestors had built structures that still stand and astonish all who see them. For it was our ancestors who built them—not the First Travelers, but the first Quespodons! The Old Earthers would have you believe that all history began with them, but that's only one more of their lies. History began with us, brothers, with the Quespodons! We were not made to serve, but to be free! We were the first! We were the best, and we shall be so again!"

The Quespodons picked up these phrases and began to chant them. The room was filled with sound and motion, and a great exhilaration. Axxal felt jubilation growing even in himself, he who had planned all this so carefully with Vaxxt. It astonished him to realize how much he had learned from Jorry, and how much better he was able to use what he had learned.

Vaxxt went on to tell the assembly what they might expect in the days to come, and how to act toward Gariv's forces in the event of trouble. When the crowd left, he and Axxal detained some dozen Quespodons, those who seemed more promising than the rest, and gave them more detailed instructions.

When all had gone, Axxal said, "We did well, don't you think so?"

Vaxxt paused before saying judiciously, "Yes. It's the first time I saw Quespodons who weren't ashamed of being what they are."

"When you mentioned the ruins, it was like . . . it was as if you had shone a light into a dark room. Suddenly they all saw the possibility that our remote ancestors had done great things," Axxal said. "Greater than even the Old Earthers."

"Perhaps they did. Since no one knows, we might as well claim them. We need them. Just as we needed your creation story."

"Do you think they believed it?"

"They didn't *want* to, not at first. They were terrified. But by the time you finished—"

"And then when you mentioned the ruins—"

"Yes, they're convinced. It was a good idea, Axxal, a very good idea, changing the old story of the Trickster that way."

Axxal thought of Jorry's subtle words aboard the *Seraph,* and said, "It was suggested to me by a very clever man."

"We owe him our thanks." Vaxxt was silent, thoughtful, and at length he said, "I heard many a legend and tale of creation in the work camp, but not until you mentioned it did I realize that of all I'd heard, only the Quespodons' made them out to be inferior. That has to be the work of others. No people debases its origins that way. Your version gives us pride."

"We were the first. We were the best," Axxal repeated.

"A good battle cry, if we should need one. I wonder if it's really true."

"I've often wondered about that. Not just about Quespodons, about all of us. Where did we all come

121

from? We're so different, and yet we're similar in so many ways . . . what can be the purpose of it all?"

"I have no answers for you."

"No. We haven't come far enough for answers, Vaxxt. But at least we're learning to ask the questions."

"Yes, we are," Vaxxt said. Then, rising, "No more time for them now, though. There's still much to be done."

VII.

The Readying

The poised quiet of midday filled the castle. Within, all was dim and cool. A faint breeze whispered through the shaded alcove in Santrahaar's chambers where she and Jorry were alone.

Her arms were tight around Jorry's waist. Her head lay on his chest. One slender tentacle caressed his cheek gently; the other touched the scar where it crossed his ribs. He stroked her soft shoulder and breathed a deep sigh of content.

"In some ways you're so like Gariv," the green girl said in her soft musical voice, "and yet you're so very different. Do your people really share the same blood?"

"It's a very distant relationship."

"Are you really a free trader, Jorry?" she asked.

He glanced at her innocently. "Of course. What else would I be? Do you think I'm a pirate?"

"You seem . . . I've seen traders before. They come to Xhancholii often. None were like you."

He laughed quietly and turned to her. "Am I better or worse?"

"You're completely different. You address Gariv as king, and yet your manner shows that you think him less than your servant."

"He doesn't seem to have noticed."

Her voice was scornful as she said, "He notices nothing." But she brightened and went on, "And you gave me a jewel—the finest jewel on this planet—as casually as if you were giving me a trinket from the market."

"I wanted you to know how I felt about you. The jewel

123

is the most beautiful thing I had ever seen, until I saw you." Jorry drew her closer to him.

They said nothing for a time, then Santrahaar said joyously, "Oh, Jorry, I'm so glad you came to Xhanchos!"

"So am I. I've never been happier, in all my travels."

"Take me away with you, Jorry," she said. "It can always be like this, just the two of us on some quiet world we choose."

"I'll take you away, if that's your wish. But Xhanchos is your homeworld, and your people can't live long away from it."

She looked up at him, her dark eyes wide and pleading. "Perhaps that's true, perhaps not. I cannot tell. But I want to go. I fear what may come."

"Gariv? He'll never find out about us."

"No, not Gariv. For all his loud words, Gariv is a little man. I fear worse things. I saw the horrors of the great battle, when the Xhanchilion were overthrown, and I fear a worse battle to come. Gariv speaks of crushing his old comrades, and I hear talk among my own servants. There will be battle soon, and we must leave before it comes." She trembled, and clutched him tightly. "Please, Jorry."

"How soon?"

"Very soon. The servants will tell me nothing—they think I'd betray them to the Skorats—but I overhear them. It will be soon, Jorry. Before the next moon cycle."

"I'll have to think of something. This will be a tricky business, Santrahaar. I can manage it, but it will be difficult."

"Can't we just slip aboard your ship while everyone sleeps? We could go now." She sprang up and tugged at Jorry's hand. "Yes, we'll go now, when there's no one to stop us!"

Jorry shook his head and pulled her to him. "It's too late. Gariv's put a three-man guard on the *Seraph*. To protect it from the rabble, he tells me."

"I could hide in something you carry aboard," she said hopefully. "I've heard tales of lovers doing such things."

He grunted, was silent for a time, and then in a slow

and thoughtful voice he said, "So you could. They'd have no reason to suspect me. And even if they do, with Axxal's help I can handle three guards and be off before anyone can stop us."

"Then you will! When, Jorry?"

"No sense in delaying. We'll never get to the *Seraph* if we have to go through a revolution. . . . Can you be ready by sunrise?"

"Oh, yes!" She brightened, and Jorry was moved once again by this beautiful woman, consort to kings, who loved him enough to risk flight and possible death. Jorry appreciated this, although he could not understand it. The k'Turalp'Pa were not a loving people. In his own distant way, Jorry felt a fondness for Santrahaar, but love was an emotion alien to him.

"Very well, then. I'll make some purchases in town after nightfall, lots of things, and have them packed in a chest big enough to hold you. I'll tell Gariv I'm bringing it aboard for safekeeping, and once we're on the *Seraph*, you'll be free of him. We're taking a chance, Santrahaar—I want you to know that."

"I take it gladly. To be free, with you . . . No Gariv, no armed men everywhere I look. Oh, Jorry, a kindly Over-being brought you to Skorat!"

Jorry laughed softly at these words. "I'm more inclined to think it was Keoffo, the Trickster. But whoever it was, I'm most grateful to him."

Jorry left Santrahaar's chamber by the little-used corridor that had become familiar to him since their first meeting. He felt something more akin to real contentment than anything he had felt at any time within memory, and once he stopped to laugh aloud from sheer good spirits. He, a k'Turalp'Pa practiced in craftiness and subtlety, was going to carry off a queen by means of a trick from the oldest legends of the oldest races. It was really quite amusing. And most appropriate, too, for his farewell to this semicivilized world. Xhanchos and its upstart monarch deserved no better at his hands.

Much had happened during Jorry's brief stay on Xhanchos, and even before Sántrahaar had spoken, he had sensed events rapidly coming to a head and begun laying his plans. He had furthered the unrest by passing on—with seeming innocence—remarks made by Gariv. Axxal could be trusted to spread the word of Gariv's plans for the rabble of the Free Army. The Quespodons and their comrades would be ready to act to preserve their newly won freedom, that was certain.

At first, Jorry had entertained a scheme for turning the Skorats and Skeggjatts against one another, raising the others against the survivors, and declaring a commonwealth. It would not be difficult to bring about. Rudstromite preachers and others were gathering crowds in the outer quarters of Xhancholii with their talk of freedom and equality, and Jorry found it to his taste. Let them have their commonwealth; Kian Jorry was the only man capable of ruling Xhanchos, and while the little men clawed at one another for their precious morsels of dignity, he could wield power in tranquility, with Santrahaar by his side, for as long as he chose before returning to Boroq-Thaddoi.

Jorry's innate appetite for intrigue was augmented by a great dislike for Gariv and his followers. They were proud, arrogant men, shrewd in some few ways and stupid in most others, and the more he saw of them, the more he heard them speak, the greater his contempt became. To be sure, their Xhanchilion predecessors had little to recommend them. From the dawn of their history, they had enslaved and driven fellow humans to death merely to raise monuments to their own vanity. When their own world did not provide criminals enough to raise the pyramids, they sought workers from all the worlds, and paid the slavers well for them.

But Gariv and his warriors were scant improvement. They were as brutal as the Xhanchilion, they held as little regard for any life not their own, and worse than the Xhanchilion, they left nothing behind them. They could only destroy.

From each side of Xhancholii, one could see a row of

blue pyramids extending into the desert. They represented a vast span of time. Now, no more would rise. When the humans of Old Earth still dwelt in caves and the vanished empire of the Tett'tu ruled four star systems; when the cold dead world of Utior and the spired cities of Anom still teemed with life, pyramids were rising on Xhanchos. Other worlds had changed. Cultures had arisen, flourished, and died, and still the Xhanchilion obeyed their strange, timeless compulsion to raise these great mounds of stone. And it was forever over. Gariv had ended slavery under the pyramid-builders, only to replace it with servitude to warriors.

Jorry felt this to be an affront. He was not particularly concerned with matters of justice and injustice, but his k'Turalp'Pa blood gave him a reverence for beauty and accomplishment. He saw Gariv's rule as a mockery. Skorats were unfit to rule. Even Quespodons, he judged, could do no worse. Perhaps lacking Skorat arrogance, they might try to preserve the best accomplishments of the Xhanchilion rather than sweep all away in a wave of destruction.

For a time, before he realized how close the Quespodons and their allies were to rising, Jorry had also contemplated a simple outright seizure of power. It could have been easily done. A stock of firearms was hidden aboard the *Seraph,* and as far as Jorry could determine, these were the only weapons on Xhanchos except for the swords and javelins of Gariv's troops. Thus armed, Jorry, Axxal, and a small band of rebels could not be withstood. Six of them could conquer a world like this one.

The lack of advanced weaponry in the galaxy, and the great disparity of arms from world to world, were glaring anomalies of intersystem travel, but few starfarers dwelt on the situation or its implications. They simply accepted existing conditions, as they accepted the powerful ships whose workings were a mystery to them. Some thoughtful men wondered at the incongruity of multilightspeed driveships manned by crews whose most powerful weapon was a cutlass or pistol; of healers who could replace a severed limb, and bloody tournaments in which men slaughtered one another by the hundreds in observance of traditions whose origin was long forgotten; of the great machine on Watson that served as repository for the legal wisdom of scores of civilizations, while on hundreds of worlds, justice was sought in the muttering of a seer or the casting of carven stones. Such things existed side by side in the same galaxy. A lightspeed traveler could go from the most sophisticated civilization to the most primitive in a single journey from system to system. This time, Jorry had thought to turn the backwardness of Xhanchos and its rulers to his advantage, and pluck an easy kingdom for himself.

But Santrahaar had prevailed upon him to abandon all such plans for mastery, and to flee with her to a new life together under far and unfamiliar stars. Jorry reflected on her suggestion, and found it appealing. He was not particularly eager for battle, even when the odds were on his side. Battle was too often a contest of luck, not wits. His luck had been uneven of late. Better not to trust to it, he judged. His share of the stones, plus whatever Santrahaar could carry off, would keep them in comfort for a long time. Eventually, he would return to Boroq-Thaddoi to complete his search for the Leddendorf ransom, but he saw no need to hurry. In all the galaxy, only Axxal shared his secret, and Jorry could not bring himself to look upon a Quespodon as a serious rival in any undertaking.

Since he and Santrahaar had become lovers, Jorry found himself prey to conflicting sensations. At first, he had wanted Santrahaar as a possession, in the way one covets any rare and beautiful object. Gafaal women were famed throughout the galaxy, and his pride drove him to seek one. When he found Santrahaar the trophy of a boorish usurper, he decided to take her for himself. It was only proper.

He considered it perfectly reasonable for her to love him and choose him over the brutish Gariv. He was the better man, and the choice was to her advantage. The fact that she so chose placed no obligations on him, as far as he could perceive, except to make the most of the situation. To take Santrahaar from Gariv would amuse him; to stay with her for a time would give them both pleasure, and would demand no sacrifice on his part. He had a long life ahead. When he tired of her company there would be ample time to return to Boroq-Thaddoi. With Leddendorf's wealth aboard his ship, he would go where he pleased, travel far and fast in pursuit of whatever lay beyond the farthest stars in that vastness still unexplored. For the time being, he would enjoy himself.

At the inn, Jorry stopped at Axxal's chamber. The Quespodon was sprawled face down on his pallet, fully dressed, deep in an exhausted sleep. It took Jorry some time to awaken him.

"I've been wondering what became of you, lad," Jorry said when his servant was awake, sitting on the edge of the pallet, yawning. "Found a girl, have you?"

"Nothing like that, Jorry."

"Well, your old captain has found the woman for him, my boy. Santrahaar, consort of the puffed-up monarch of Xhanchos. I'm taking her off this planet at sunrise, and I'll need your help."

"I'll help if I can, Jorry, but I'm not leaving."

"What in the blazing rings do you mean by that?" Jorry roared. "You're a crewman on the *Seraph,* and I'm the captain, and when I give an order you'll obey it."

"But you don't need me, Jorry, and they do, all the Quespodons here really need me. I can't leave them now."

"Can't leave them *now?*" Jorry repeated. He gave Axxal a suspicious look, then pulled a low chair to him and seated himself facing the pallet. "What are you involved in, Axxal?" he asked.

Axxal fumbled at an explanation. "I've gotten to know—we're trying to—to make the Quespodons and all the rest . . . They must realize that if they don't try to protect themselves . . ." He looked awkwardly at Jorry and fell silent.

Jorry's voice was cool, his words direct. "Some people around the palace think there may be an uprising. When will it take place, Axxal?"

"I don't know. Very soon, but I don't know exactly. I'll help you get away, Jorry, but my place is here."

Jorry frowned thoughtfully, nodded, then broke into a grin. "It looks as though the captain's orderly has grown up. You're a man now, Axxal, and I can't take a man from his proper business. Especially when I think it's worthwhile. Ordinarily, I'd have been pleased to lend a hand, but lately I'm not the same old Captain Jorry. Tell me, how are you armed? You're taking on a tough bunch of warriors, you know."

"We have a few good blades. Some Thorumbians are working on longbows, and we have men making swords, but most of our force will be armed with clubs. We have the advantage of numbers, and surprise will be on our side."

Jorry shook his head. "Don't count on that. Gariv must have spies among your men. He knows a lot."

Axxal looked disturbed at this news. When Jorry had given him more details, he said, "If Gariv knows when and where we plan to strike, he'll wipe us out."

"Not necessarily," Jorry said, his attitude that of a parent, or a tutor. "Unless I'm greatly mistaken, you've been doing a good bit of thinking lately. Think harder. Think of what's aboard the *Seraph*."

Axxal furrowed his brow in deep concentration, tugged at an ear, then brightened and cried, "Guns!"

"Right you are. I'll want to keep two brace of pistols for my own peace of mine. The rest is yours—"

"Jorry, that's what we—"

"—in return for your share of the stones," Jorry went on. "Fair enough?" When Axxal hesitated, he chided him, "Those weapons will give you Xhanchos, my lad. I'm asking a small price for a world."

"You are, Jorry. I agree."

"Smart lad. You've learned a lot from my example," Jorry said, rising and stretching. "I'm going to rest for a while. Tonight I'll make a few purchases. Meet me here at sunrise. And wherever you go tonight, stay out of trouble. Once I'm aloft you can blow this place apart, Axxal, but until then, take care."

VIII.

The Judgment of Gariv

Jorry had been in difficult situations often enough in his life to have learned the value of self-possession and the usefulness of the calm exterior in times of trial. When the pair of armed Skeggjatts appeared at the inn late in the night, therefore, he greeted them amiably and apologized for the disarray of his chamber. He was repacking some goods, and that was always a messy business, especially when one's servant is off somewhere. . . .

But they were not there to inspect his quarters or to chat: They had come to conduct him to the monarch's presence on a matter of great urgency. Jorry wondered at this, but he had no choice; he went with them.

Gariv dismissed the guards as soon as Jorry entered the throne room. He looked quite perturbed. He was wearing armor over his trunk and arms, and his helmet and sword lay by the throne. In a tense voice, he said, "The rising will be tonight. I'm sure of it."

Jorry felt a surge of annoyance at being dragged away from his own concerns on the mere whim of an apprehensive king; but he checked his feelings and spoke politely. "I was in the city most of the night, purchasing goods, and I saw no signs of trouble. Why does Your Majesty expect the rising now?"

"That green witch has been meeting someone secretly."

"Santrahaar?" Jorry broke in, amazed.

"Yes, Santrahaar, my consort. She's been passing information to my enemies since the day I freed her."

"That's impossible!"

Gariv turned on him angrily. "Don't tell me what's impossible, trader. My guards saw someone leaving the palace last midday. They traced the corridor he used— one that we were unaware of—and found a concealed entrance to Santrahaar's chambers. I went to speak to her of this when I awoke, and found her preparing to slip out of the castle to safety while her army of rabble besieged the palace."

It could not have been a stratagem. Gariv did not have the craft for it. Skorat style required a direct accusation, delivered in a shout, before a large group. This was no snare for Jorry, but something else, something quite unexpected and unplanned for. Jorry had to know more.

"Are you sure she was running to your enemies? She might have been going to her lover."

Gariv stared at him in disbelief. "Her lover? No man on this planet would dare look at her."

"I've looked at her many times."

The response was contemptuous. "You're a trader. I'm speaking of men, warriors. Santrahaar was bred to recognize greatness. Where would she turn but to me?"

"What did you do with her, Gariv?"

"I killed her. What else would I do? I freed her, let her sit at my side, and she betrayed me."

Jorry drew a sharp breath, held it for a moment with his gaze fixed on the Monarch of Xhanchos, and let out a long sigh. Once again his hopes and plans had been thwarted by the stupidity of others. Slowly, in a hushed voice devoid of intonation, like a man repeating some impossible news to himself, he said, "So Santrahaar is dead."

"What is it to you, trader?"

"I wanted her for myself." When Gariv's laughter had died away, Jorry went on, "And she loved me. She was coming to meet me at sunrise. We planned to leave this planet that you and your lackeys mean to turn into an arena. But you've killed her, and that's all over."

"You lie, trader. Santrahaar was mine. She wouldn't allow you to touch the dust she walked on."

Jorry saw no further need to dissemble. "Does it hurt your Skorat pride to think of her in my arms? In that

133

case, you've been deeply injured, many times. I'm almost tempted to pity you, but I can't. I can only despise you." Jorry folded his arms and looked Gariv up and down. "You do wrong to speak of yourself as a great man, Gariv. Men such as you may seize power by killing those who possess it; you may even retain it for a little while, as if you were truly fit to rule. But greatness is beyond you."

"Enough, trader. I don't like your talk."

"You'd like it even less if you had the brains to understand it. The only greatness you'll ever know, Gariv, is the greatness of your own folly. In one day, you killed the most beautiful woman on this world and threw away your throne. And your life."

"You insult me. You dare to threaten me!"

"I recite facts. If you choose to be insulted or threatened, so much the worse for you."

In a single swift move, Gariv rose and snatched up his sword. "I had you brought here to offer you the chance of fighting on the winning side, trader. I could easily cut you down where you stand," he said ominously.

Jorry looked at him, half-smiling. "You sent for me because you're afraid. One more sword wielded in your defense, even though it's in the hands of a trader—that's all you want. But I'll not fight for you, and you'll not cut me down. I'm going to kill you, Gariv. And then I'm going to arm the Quespodons and their allies and turn them loose against your men."

Gariv was silent for a moment, weighing this, and then he laughed aloud. "How will you kill me, trader? With words? With your bare hands?" He raised the blade, slashed showily to his left and right, then steadied the point an arm's length from Jorry's throat. "If you have a weapon, use it, trader," he said.

Jorry slipped a small blade into each hand. At the sight of them, Gariv spat. "A man uses a sword, trader," he said contemptuously.

Jorry's voice was weary, like that of a man speaking to an unruly child. "This isn't a tournament. I don't mean to do battle with you, I mean to execute you."

Gariv drew back a step. "I'll waste no time on you. One stroke and you'll be slit in two. Do you hear me? I've done it to better men, scores of them. Hundreds of them. And you . . . with your feeble finger knives . . ."

Jorry shook his head and sighed, as if reluctant to do what he must. "You're consistent to the end, Gariv. Blustering, bragging, and utterly stupid." He raised his hands to the aiming position. Gariv drew back his sword and lunged forward. A single snap of Jorry's wrist and the Skorat tumbled over the dais and fell at Jorry's feet. Over his left eye, almost invisible under the thick brow, was a small hole. His sword hand twitched twice, convulsively, then he shuddered and lay still.

Jorry kicked the sword away, lifted the body, and propped it on the throne. From a short distance, it looked as if the Monarch of Xhanchos were deep in thought. Jorry turned to leave, and his eye fell on the motion painting of Nikkolope. He picked it up, placed it in his tunic, and went to the doors, instructing the guards that Gariv did not wish to be disturbed. Then he set out for the inn, where Axxal was waiting.

When Jorry entered the chamber, something in his manner made Axxal hesitant to speak. With a gesture, he signaled the Quespodon to a seat, then took a stance facing him, his back to the closed door.

"Answer me this, Axxal, and tell the truth: Was Santrahaar spying for your people all along?" he demanded.

"The consort of Gariv, our spy? No, Jorry," Axxal answered, puzzled but earnest.

"How certain can you be?"

"Her name was never mentioned. I would have heard it. We had five spies in the palace, all Xhanchilion. She never helped us."

Jorry folded his arms and leaned back against the door. "Gariv believed she was spying on him. He found her ready to leave the palace, and he believed she was on her way to safety before the attack."

"But she was going to meet *you*. He was wrong."

"Wrong or not, he killed her."

135

Axxal was stunned by the statement, and the flat, colorless tone in which it was delivered. He looked up at Jorry and repeated softly, "Killed her?"

"Yes. So I killed him. I wanted Santrahaar and he killed her. Gariv is propped up on the throne of Xhanchos now, and I dare say he'll rule as wisely as he did before. Once the body is found, the castle will be in a turmoil. Get to your people and tell them to attack this day without fail. The Skorats and Skeggjatts will be leaderless. You'll be able to wipe them out to the last man."

"The weapons," Axxal reminded him.

"You'll have them. Come with me, now."

Axxal looked around the room, where trade goods lay in scattered profusion. A large chest gaped empty in the middle of the chamber. "What of all this?" he asked.

"No use to me now. Come."

Jorry led the way briskly through the quiet streets of the palace quarter, displayed the royal token at the gate and was passed by the guards, and proceeded to the *Seraph*. One guard rose languidly from his place in the shadow of the ship and signaled the two traders to halt.

"What's your business?" he demanded.

"I have orders from Gariv, monarch of Xhanchos. He wants certain articles brought from the ship," Jorry responded.

"It's early in the day, trader. No time to work."

"Gariv wants the things at once. I'm no happier than you are to be working under the sun, friend, but I'll not dispute his orders. Will you?"

The guard muttered under his breath and started for the shelter where the others rested. Jorry followed him inside. He emerged from the shelter alone.

Once aboard the *Seraph*, Axxal and Jorry quickly readied a pack with the rifles, six pistols, and an ample stock of ammunition. It was quite heavy, but Axxal swung it to his shoulder with ease.

"I'll circle around the city and enter by the Dark Gate," he said. "We know a way past the guards. But you must go now."

"No fear of my staying. I have little taste for this world. Good luck to you, Axxal."

"Thanks, Jorry. Good luck to you, on Boroq-Thaddoi."

Jorry shook his head. "My luck's been poor of late, Axxal. Maybe your Trickster has decided to adopt me, now that he's lost his Quespodons." He laughed drily. "I'll manage him, though. I know a trick or two myself. I hope you've learned a few."

"You've taught me much, Jorry."

"You were a good pupil. You have the makings of a first-rate starfarer in you, lad. I'll give you one last chance—do you want to forget all the politics and return to Boroq-Thaddoi with me? We'll pick a choice crew. This time, we'll go right in by the back door, and have no traps to worry about. It's just a matter of digging through the rubble, now."

"I'd like that, Jorry, but I can't leave my brothers. I have to stay."

"I suppose you do. So there's nothing left but to get the *Seraph* aloft and clear the ring for the Daltrescans. They'll have a lively time when they land with the next shipment of slaves."

"Very lively," Axxal agreed.

"And you're sure you can handle a ship that size? It won't be like the *Seraph,* you know."

"I can do it, Jorry. What I don't know, I'll have the Daltrescans show me. They'll be glad to co-operate, once we've finished with them."

Jorry nodded with satisfaction. "You've learned a few things, that's plain. Learn one more: Let others do the fighting, while you make the plans. You'll live much longer. Now be on your way, and I'll be on mine."

From the skimpy shade of a shallow ravine, Axxal heard the shrill whine of a drivecoil. He turned in time to see the *Seraph* flash upward. Jorry was gone. Axxal was alone now, a leader among his own people, no man's servant.

IX

The Leader of the Quespodons

First Axxal concealed the weapons. This done, he slumped to the cool stone floor to recover his strength, sapped by exposure to the Xhanchilion desert sun. He lay motionless for a time, exhausted, thinking.

Rest was a luxury he could not afford, and he well knew this. Much lay ahead of him, and no time could be spared. By nightfall, warfare might be raging in the streets as rival forces battled for dominion. Jorry had spoken of six distinct factions within the Skorat camp alone. Axxal knew of that many, and more, among the outsiders. The final clash was near at hand. Vaxxt had to be informed, plans had to be made, weapons distributed. Soon the Quespodons and their supporters would hold Xhancholii. Many might fall, but they would prevail.

Axxal lay still, his breathing quiet now, and reflected on the prospect. The more deeply he considered it, the less it satisfied him. The thought came that Xhancholii might require a high price. If the Quespodon forces were too much diminished in taking the city, then victory might leave them too weak to seize the Daltrescan driveship. If they were forced to remain on this world, even as its lords, all their efforts would have been wasted.

There had to be alternatives. Axxal sought to reason them out.

With Gariv dead and powerful weapons in the hands of the Quespodons, there was a chance of avoiding a clash. Skorats were a warrior race, true, and instinct would lead them to draw the sword; but now, divided and demoralized, their leader struck down on his very throne by an unknown hand, even they might choose parley over battle with a strong and well-armed enemy. It was worth the attempt.

Axxal turned the idea over in his mind. Perhaps the Quespodons could, after all, achieve their aims without a battle against the warriors from the palace. Before them lay one inevitable clash: Blood would flow when the slavers' driveship landed, and there was no avoiding it. Freedmen of every breed had memories of their treatment at Daltrescan hands.

The ship must be taken, and taken intact. Then, if Gariv's successors wanted the city—indeed, the whole planet—they were welcome to it. The Quespodons must have the driveship. They *would* have it, whatever the cost. But if the cost in Quespodon lives could be reduced, so much the better.

Axxal climbed to his feet. His head ached from thought, and this was only the beginning. His expression, as he walked the shaded alleys and byways of Xhancholii, was solemn. He was grappling with a problem far more complex, seeking solutions far more elusive, than the clean logical workings of a driveship. He was trying to build the future of his people.

When at last he reached Vaxxt, drew him apart into a private corner and gave him news of Gariv's death, the other Quespodon reacted in an odd way. Axxal had expected excitement, a rallying cry, a call to arms. His chief fear had been that Vaxxt would stir up their forces to action before he could present his own arguments. But Vaxxt was strangely silent. It seemed almost as though the removal of Gariv distressed him.

In the face of Vaxxt's reluctance, Axxal grew more confident in his own plans. The other leaders were summoned and as each heard his story, they turned to Vaxxt for a decision. No decision came. Axxal felt a great urgency gnawing at him, but he forced himself to be patient. The right moment had not yet come.

"What are we to do, Vaxxt?" one of the others pressed.

139

"We can't delay much longer. We have to move by night-fall."

"I know, I know," their leader replied impatiently. But he said no more, and he did not move. The others began to speak out more boldly.

"I say we fight. Attack now, while they're confused."

"A good idea. They won't expect an attack by day."

"We've always talked of rising against Gariv's forces—now is our chance."

Vaxxt gestured angrily for silence. "Give me time to think, will you? We can't just . . . just rush headlong on the palace. We'd lose too many lives."

These were the words Axxal had been awaiting, and he pounced on them. "Then why risk any Quespodon lives? We can get what we want without fighting. Then we'll be able to turn our full strength against the slavers when they land," he said.

"That's true. We have to think about the ship," one of the others said.

"We have to think *first* of the ship," Axxal corrected him. "That's more important than anything else."

"What's your suggestion?" Vaxxt asked.

"Negotiate."

Vaxxt's eyes blazed, and in his anger he spoke with the passion of his old self. "Negotiate?! We're Quespodons, Axxal—you forget that too easily."

"I have not forgotten what I am."

"Then what makes you think that others would deal honestly and truthfully with us? No one negotiates with Quespodons. They use our strength, they rob our world of its wealth, but deal with us as equals? Never! Never have they done this, and never will they!" Vaxxt said forcefully.

"They would deal honestly with us now, because they have no choice," Axxal said in a calm voice. "Consider: the palace is filled with fear and confusion. No one knows who can be trusted and who is to be feared."

"All the more reason to strike now!"

Axxal turned to the one who had spoken. "I think not.

140

That might unite them against us. Even with our weapons, that would mean a hard fight and heavy losses."

"That is true," the speaker admitted. Others nodded in agreement.

Axxal went on, "We can speak for a unified force of Quespodons. We are armed and ready to fight, but only if we must. We need not promise to support anyone. It will be enough if we promise to aid no one."

"Why would they believe us?"

"I think they would. Anyway, does it matter? What they want is not what we want. Let them have Xhancholii, and we will take the ship."

Someone asked, "But will they give us the ship?"

"The Daltrescan ship is not theirs to give. It belongs to those who take it, and we can take it if our forces are not diminished by a battle for a city we wish only to leave. What we must do . . ." Axxal paused, groping for words to formuate his thoughts, then proceeded, "We must convince them that it's to their advantage to get us off Xhanchos. We must make them think that this is their idea, and not ours. Let them think they're deceiving us, if it helps our cause. They're Skorats; if they think we want the ship, *they'll* want it. So they must think that we do not. Do you understand?"

Vaxxt looked at him with new respect. "You've learned much of otherworlders' ways. This is a dangerous game to play."

"There is no other way."

"No. But it will be difficult. We're Quespodons, Axxal, not otherworlders. We have no skill in . . . in saying things we know to be untrue, or acting in ways we do not feel," Vaxxt said uneasily. "Perhaps, until we learn these things . . . perhaps it would be best to trust in our strength. We have weapons . . ." He looked at Axxal submissively, almost apologizing for his words.

When he saw that expression, Axxal understood all the hesitation and the reluctance to act: the crisis had arrived, and Vaxxt was not ready. Perhaps he would never be ready to act, however skilled he might be at rousing

141

others to action. Axxal knew that the leadership of the Quespodons had passed to him, and he spoke decisively.

"It's time we began to learn the otherworlders' tricks, Vaxxt, but we won't become like them. We're not a race of warriors, like the Skorats, and I would not make us such a race. First, we'll try to deal in peace. If that fails, we can turn to our weapons."

His words impressed the others, and they accepted his suggestion without further debate. "Who will you speak with among the palace forces? You said yourself that they're divided," Vaxxt said.

"I know which group is most likely to win. I'll go to their leader."

Another asked, "Will he listen to you, Axxal? Can you trust a Skorat?"

Axxal remembered Jorry's words. "He will listen. Skorats always back down before someone who shows no fear. And I will not be fool enough to trust them."

"One thing more," said Vaxxt, rising and hobbling before the group. "You must go at once, and without me. Warrior races have no regard for a cripple, and you'll do better if I'm not with you."

"But you always speak for us!" one of the others objected, and a second asked, "Who will deal with the Skorats if we leave you behind?"

"Axxal speaks as well as I. This is his plan."

A third Quespodon, older than the rest, by name Tumuxxat, said gruffly, "You hurt your leg in the battle for Xhanchos. You have a right to be with us, and no Skorat will dare to show you disrespect."

"This is true," Axxal said, "but we must be wary. If all our leaders are together, the Skorats might risk killing us. Then the Quespodons would be leaderless. Let Vaxxt and the others stay here. Tumuxxat and I will go to the castle now, and return by nightfall."

"If you don't return?"

"Gather the weapons and come for us."

X.

The Parley

No guard stood at the gate, but activity in the castle was unusually brisk at a time when it had been the custom to rest. The two Quespodons passed unchallenged along a succession of corridors until they came to the chambers of Ninos, where two Skorats with drawn swords barred their way.

Ignoring their challenge, Axxal said, "I'm here to see your master on a matter of great importance to him. Bring me to him at once."

"Tell me what this matter is, Quespodon. I'll judge whether or not you see him," one guard said.

"I'll tell you nothing. I've come to see Ninos, not his guards."

The Skorat eyed the two uncertainly. He was not accustomed to such a reaction from Quespodons. Tumuxxat stayed close to Axxal, fidgeting with mixed pride and apprehension. It was good to see one of his own people speak so boldly to a Skorat, but he could scarcely believe that they were not going to be cut down on the spot for such insolence. Instead, within a very short time, they were taken to Ninos.

He received them as if they were two old friends. Tumuxxat and the guard were equally bewildered by the reception, but it did not surprise Axxal. He had expected something like this from an ambitious man. Jorry was a good judge of people, and it was Jorry who had predicted that when events on Xhanchos had run their course, if only one person remained alive, that person would be a shrewd and wily Skorat named Ninos. It was with Jorry's words in mind that Axxal had come to this man, and he now studied him closely.

Ninos was ingratiating in manner, unctuous in speech. He listened carefully, responding quickly but with vague words to whatever was said. His mind was very busy. Axxal knew that he was dealing with a clever and resourceful man. Jorry might think him an amusing fool— but Jorry was a k'Turalp'Pa with a lifetime of intrigue behind him. Axxal was new at this sort of thing. The only factor in his favor was that while he was aware of the shrewdness of Ninos and his own limitations, the Skorat was convinced that he was a brilliant man dealing with nearly mindless Quespodons. Axxal did not hope to deceive Ninos, but he knew that it might not be necessary. Such men as Ninos deceive themselves.

Ninos dismissed the guard and signaled for his guests to seat themselves. At his bidding, two servants entered, one bearing a tray of spiced fruits, the other a decanter. They placed these before the Quespodons and withdrew without speaking.

"You've traveled through the heat at an unaccustomed hour," Ninos said, pouring a pale yellow liquid from the decanter into two tiny cups, "and you must need refreshment. Drink this, and take a morsel, and then we will talk."

Wary of Skorat treachery, the Quespodons raised the cups to their lips without drinking and forebore to sample the tray of fruits. They sat in silence as Ninos talked on, in a manner and tone so disarming that they kept their guard up only by a conscious effort to remember where they were and why they had come. At last their host came to the matter at hand.

"My duties at the palace have prevented me from meeting more of the Quespodons," he said, and his expression attested to his deep regret at this omission. "I've long wanted to know you better. I saw how boldly you fought when we took the city—indeed, were it not for the courage and sacrifices of the Quespodon, the Free Army could never have taken Xhancholii, although few of my

144

fellow Skorats will admit as much. I've made my share of enemies among them by daring to speak out on your people's behalf. But now you've come to see me, and by your own words, on a matter of some importance. I'm glad. That shows trust, and I want your trust, as well as your friendship. Now tell me, Axxal, Tumuxxat, what Ninos can do for his friends."

Axxal hesitated, then cleared his throat nervously before he spoke. He wanted to appear ill at ease, uncertain and groping for a course of action some wiser man might suggest. Abruptly, he leaned forward and blurted, "Captain Jorry was my partner."

Ninos appeared puzzled for a moment, then brightened. "Ah, yes, the trader. Or so he called himself. And what of him?"

"He's gone. He left Xhanchos."

Ninos weighed the news in silence. Axxal remained impassive. In the heavy midday silence, he could almost hear the furious working of the Skorat's mind as he calculated the implications of Jorry's flight. After a time, Ninos asked, "Why have you come to me, Axxal? I'm pleased to have your trust, you must know that, but you don't know me, and yet you've come here."

"Jorry once said that after Gariv, you would rule."

"Did he, indeed?"

"Yes. He said there would be much blood shed, but you would become the monarch of Xhanchos."

Ninos smiled. "Then Gariv is truly dead."

"Jorry slew him. They fought over the Gafaal woman."

The Skorat leaned back and laughed softly to himself. "How very appropriate," he said happily. "And how convenient. Gariv dead, Jorry gone . . . you're sure of this?"

"Jorry told me so."

"I see. It explains much that has taken place since sunrise."

"When you rule, Ninos, we want you to be our friend," Axxal said.

Ninos beamed upon them and spread his arms wide, betokening generosity. "I shall be friend and father to the

145

Quespodons, I assure you. You've brought me valuable information at a most opportune time, and I shall make the most of it."

"Will blood be shed?"

Ninos made a negligent gesture. "A bit. A handful of men must be removed, no more. Tell me this, Axxal—if I should need support, can I count on the Quespodons?"

Axxal frowned, as if thinking deeply on his answer. He tugged at his ear, shook his head, and slowly replied, "I think not. This is what Gariv wanted, but our leaders would not agree."

"So that's why Gariv was so friendly with the trader—he used him to deal with the Quespodons through you."

"Yes. But my people trust no one in the palace. Even now, when they have arms—"

"Arms? What arms do they have?" Ninos broke in sharply.

"Clubs, mostly. A few blades. Some pistols and rifles, with ammunition."

"Where did they get firearms?"

"Jorry gave them to us when he left."

Ninos drew the two Quespodons closer and spoke in a low, confidential tone. "These firearms can be very important to us, my friends. We must arrange for my forces to have them. Do you know where they are, Tumuxxat?"

"Hidden," the Quespodon replied.

"But where? Axxal, do you know?"

Axxal shook his head. "They took them from Jorry and hid them outside, in the desert. No one would tell us where. The Quespodon leaders say they will use them only to defend themselves, not to fight for others."

Ninos nodded thoughtfully and broke away from them to pace the floor. Axxal sensed his deliberations and said in a strained, halting voice, "They don't want . . . none of us want to fight for Xhancholii. It belongs to the Skorat by right of conquest. But we don't. We've finally got freedom, and we want to keep it."

"I understand perfectly," Ninos murmured.

"If we could leave, we'd do so gladly."

Axxal waited, looking into Ninos' face, hoping the Skorat would take the bait. His tactics could easily go wrong. If the Skorats suspected that others were aware of the impending arrival of the Daltrescan ship and hoped to seize it, they would lay claim to it themselves out of sheer willfulness. But if they could toss it to a lesser breed in an easy gesture of magnanimity, they might do so. Axxal counted on the latter.

Ninos stopped his pacing and looked full at the two Quespodons. His manner was that of one who has reached a difficult decision. "Your leaders are wise," he said solemnly. "They'd be fools to battle for any cause but their own. If they have no wish to possess Xhancholii, why fight for it?"

"But there is fear. . . ," Tumuxxat began.

"Speak freely, my friend. What do you fear?"

The two Quespodons exchanged uneasy glances. Tumuxxat rubbed his hairless head, then said, "We heard that Gariv planned to enslave us, and we fear that his successor might do the same."

"Then we would have to fight. We would use the weapons," Axxal said.

"Why, of course. You'd have no choice," Ninos agreed.

Tumuxxat added, "The others have said this, too. The Trulbans and Zotaron would join us."

"And the Agyari, and the Thorumbians, and even the Xhanchilion who survive," Axxal said. "Those of Gilead, too." Turning to Ninos, Axxal explained, "This is why we came to you. We must know what to expect if you become ruler of the city."

Ninos pondered, then declared, "You've acted wisely, my friends. I think I can solve all our problems. You say your people wish only to leave Xhancholii?"

"Yes!"

"Would you leave the planet entirely? All of you?"

"But we have no ship, Ninos!"

"There will be a ship. I promise you that," Ninos said. "Are you willing to fight for it?"

"We will fight for a ship, Ninos," Tumuxxat assured him.

"Then ready yourselves. The Daltrescans will arrive very soon with a cargo of slaves. Capture their ship and I give it to you, with my permission to leave Xhanchos."

Axxal looked puzzled. "But Gariv told everyone that the Daltrescans were not coming."

"And I tell you they are. Gariv lied. Trust me, and be ready."

"We will," they said.

"In return, I ask only one thing of you: Give your allegiance to no one, whatever they promise. I don't ask you to fight on my side, but you must not support anyone else. Will you agree?"

"I can only promise to tell this to our leaders. But I think this is what they want."

"I think so, too, Axxal, and I depend on them. We must trust one another. In a few days, we will all have what we most desire—you, your ship, and I, Xhancholii. Go now, and bring my promise to your people."

The Quespodons kept their part of the bargain. Ninos, assured of neutrality by those beyond the palace walls, turned all his forces against the enemies within. By nightfall of that very day the rival factions were leaderless, and before the Xhanchilion sun rose again, Ninos was established as Gariv's successor, monarch of Xhanchos and lord of the city.

On the third day of his reign, the Daltrescans landed.

XI.

Arrival and Departure

Secured on the landing ring, the Daltrescan craft loomed over the walls of Xhancholii and reached halfway to the top of the highest tower in the city. It was a massive structure, a First Stage driveship constructed on Old Earth to carry ninety-four families and all their provisions across light-millennia of uncharted space to a world no Earthly eyes had ever seen. The ship was six centuries old, scarred, bleached, and pockmarked from long voyaging; but it had centuries of service ahead. The men of those half-legendary times had built for eternity.

Now the ship carried a cargo of slaves. They had been seized in hit-and-run raids on sparsely settled planets far from the main galactic centers—agricultural worlds like Gilead and Cadzia, mining outposts on Dlugas III and Ekk, or Dumabb-Paraxx. Some had been taken from unarmed pilgrim ships, and a few were members of outlaw bands betrayed and sold by their comrades. All they had in common was their misery, and the knowledge that they were on their way to some destination where no man or woman went freely.

The main port swung open. The ramp emerged, sank, and settled firmly in the sand. Four burly Daltrescans descended and the span shook under their heavy tread. Their heads were big, set solidly on thick necks and covered with hair as coarse and bristly as a tormagon's pelt. They wore leather jerkins covered with metal plates, shaggy fur trousers, and heavy boots. Each carried a pointed prod just under a meter in length. The four took up guard positions at the foot of the ramp, two on either side, and waited.

As was the custom, shelters had been erected on the sands near the landing ring. On this occasion, the shelters were considerably larger and more numerous than they had been in the recent past, but the slavers took no notice of such details. Nor were they troubled by the darkness at the base of the city walls, where torches had always burned for their arrival. The Daltrescans dealt with many races, on many worlds. None was their friend, but none threatened them, for they trafficked in a necessary item.

Their captain, Ruklin, followed by two personal guards, came noisily down the ramp and stood awaiting the delegation from Xhancholii. It seemed to him to be rather larger than the one sent on their last visit, and he remarked on this to no one in particular.

"They fear us, Captain," one guard said. "They expect us to snatch them up and sell them to a pleasure house on Barbary."

Another laughed and said, "A small price we'd get from a pleasure house for one of these."

"We'd get it for one of their Gafaal beauties," said the first.

"Enough talk," Ruklin growled, and the rest were silent.

The merchants drew nearer. Each rode in an open litter borne on the shoulders of four big Quespodons. This was a mark of status, and not necessity; two Quespodons could easily have carried the entire group. Behind the litters trailed an entourage of servants, guards, and overseers. Six pairs of litters crossed the sand, and the twelve conveyances were lowered and lined up a short distance before the ramp.

"They're trying to impress us, Captain," one slaver said.

"That they are," a second agreed. "Brought half their slaves along."

"All they've done so far is raise my price," said Ruklin. The Daltrescans laughed among themselves, but at once resumed their sober silence as the Xhanchilion leader, having spoken briefly with the others in his party, approached them on foot, alone. He was followed at a respectful distance by two bearers. Salutations were brusque; both sides were here for business.

"I have good stock for you this time," Ruklin said. "We took a pilgrim ship. They're young and strong."

"Excellent. We've lost many since your last call," the Xhanchilion informed him.

"We've had losses, too. The pilgrims fought hard. I lost three hands, and three more wounded. That raises my price."

"You will be paid."

"And we took five stonemasons in a raid on Droxiglion," Ruklin added. "They ought to be worth plenty."

"Perhaps. They must be good."

"They're good. This time we want the red stones in payment. Nothing else, just the red stones, and we want bigger ones than you gave before."

The Xhanchilion paused. His slablike face betrayed no emotion as he considered Ruklin's demand, then he raised a hand and said, "I must confer with the others."

"What's there to confer about? Either you pay us as we demand, or you can try to get your own slaves."

The Xhanchilion gave the gesture of conciliation. "I am aware. We must confer to decide who is to return to the treasury and who will remain. You will have the red stones."

"Tell them to hurry. We don't unload until I see the red stones. Not one slave without them," Ruklin said.

He folded his arms and looked on coldly as the Xhanchilion spoke with his companions. Their high, chirping speech carried to him, but the meaning was unintelligible. Ruklin felt contempt for these effete, slab-faced city dwellers, isolated on their dry, wasted world, building monuments to their own impotence on the empty desert. A good thing they were in the buyer's role—they'd be worthless as slaves.

Was it that he was getting older? he wondered, or were

all the Xhanchilion merchants mere boys? They seemed younger than any he had dealt with before. Not a full-grown man among them. And all those servants and bearers . . . Weak and soft, that's what they were. Well, it was good for business. Let them have a score of litter bearers each, as long as Ruklin's ship supplied them.

The group separated. Six turned back, on foot, toward the city gate. Five remained. The leader returned to the Daltrescan captain.

"They go to bring the red stones, but they insist that you begin to unload the slaves at once," he informed Ruklin.

"I told you, not until I see the stones."

"The stones will be our best. The smallest one will be too big to fit into your hand. But you must begin to unload now."

Ruklin thought of the price such stones would bring on any of a score of worlds, and his resolution wavered. But easy accommodation was not in his nature. "Why the hurry?" he asked.

"You must have noticed that my companions are young, as I am. We are undertaking the purchase of replacements for the first time, and we—"

"Where are the grown men?" Ruklin interrupted.

"In the city. They will do as we decide, and evaluate our work later. My comrades insist on your unloading in order to show their firmness. They can also show generosity."

Ruklin found that final statement to his liking. He turned and signaled for the unloading to begin.

The Daltrescan ship, silent and lifeless-seeming until now, at once became a scene of great activity. A light blazed from the main port, and a discordant mingling of groans, cries, and shouted commands issued forth, growing steadily louder until the first of the captives was thrust to the ramp.

The slaves were chained together in groups of varying size. The first group, numbering six, was conveyed by six Quespodons to a shelter, for inspection. The Daltrescan guards remained below, near the ramp. Other groups of guards and slaves descended; some of the Daltrescans returned to the ship when they had delivered their charges, and others waited about, close to the ramp, in tight clusters.

Ruklin looked on as the work proceeded. Now and then he issued a command, or laid his prod across the shoulders of a lagging slave or careless guard, but for the most part unloading went smoothly. One hundred and nine slaves were delivered, of which one hundred and two were fit for work.

"Come to my shelter and we will discuss payment," said the young Xhanchilion.

"Where are the stones? You've got your slaves, but I've seen no one come from the city. What's the delay?" Ruklin demanded.

"They come now. Look." Past the Xhanchilion's pointing finger, a string of tiny figures made their way across the sand from the farthest corner of the city walls.

"Why do they come that way?"

"Shorter and faster. We wish only to save you valuable time," was the reply. "Will you come with me?"

Inside the shelter, Ruklin seated himself at a low table covered with counting tiles. The Xhanchilion took the place opposite him. At either hand, to his rear, Quespodon servants stood in attendance. Ruklin's personal guards waited outside, on either side of the entry.

"You say I've brought seven you can't use? You're being choosy," Ruklin said.

"They have been severely beaten. Two might recover, but the rest are of no use to us."

"That's *your* problem. The agreement was that you'd take all we could bring you."

The Xhanchilion raised a hand and corrected him. "All who are fit to work. You must be more careful."

"We're careful. Those seven gave us trouble." Ruklin was silent for a time, then he said, "I'll agree to this: Take the two who can recover, and put the other five to death now, before we leave. That makes a hundred and four." The Xhanchilion agreed to this, and Ruklin boasted, "I could have sold every one of these on Tarquin VII. The arena's busy these days. I'm being very generous with you."

"Indeed?"

"I sold all the women on Barbary. Every one of them, young and old. The ship's empty now. But not for long."

"No, not for long," said a slow voice behind him.

Ruklin turned and saw a Quespodon standing just inside the entry. In either hand he held a prod. The Daltrescan took a grip on his own prod and reached for the dagger in his belt. "What's this?" he demanded, rising, turning to face the others. "One of your slaves has gone crazy."

"There are no more slaves on Xhanchos," said one of the other Quespodons, stepping forward.

"Soon, no more slavers," said another.

Outside arose a great uproar, the clash of weapons and the cries of men in battle. All was clear to Ruklin. He lunged for the entry, slashing at the Quespodon who blocked his way. His arm was seized in an immobilizing grip. A blocklike fist crashed into his face. He staggered, and the prod was wrenched from his hand. A blow to his kidneys jerked him upright in pain, then he fell to his knees and crumpled to the ground under a steady merciless battering from three steel-tipped prods.

On the open sands before the city, under the fleeting minor moons, Daltrescans fought for their lives against men they had once delivered into bondage. The struggle was brief and bloody and without mercy on either side. The slavers, desperate, wielded their prods with deadly skill, but the Quespodons could not be withstood. They overwhelmed the Daltrescans on the ground. By sheer strength, they held the ramp down when those safely aboard tried to raise it. They forced their way onto the ship through a barrier of flailing, thrusting prods. The battle crept from deck to deck of the great ship, but after the first attacker won through to the control room, the outcome was settled. It was simply a question of time.

154

The faint glow of approaching day lay on the horizon when Tumuxxat, leader of the attack force, descended the ramp. One side of his face was puffed and bruised; blood trickled from his ear and swollen lips. Without a word, he lifted high a blood-smeared Daltrescan prod and then, with a swift motion, snapped it in half and tossed the fragments to the sand. "It is ours!" he cried, in a voice that carried to the walls.

A stream of bruised and bloodied Quespodons began to circulate. They carried Daltrescan bodies from the ship and then made their way back up the ramp, each assisting or carrying a wounded comrade. Every living Quespodon, even those who clearly could not survive past sunrise, was brought aboard. Their total number was ninety-eight.

When Ninos rode through the Gate of the Ring with a force of one hundred and twenty picked warriors to lay claim to the spoils of battle, the growing light revealed a bloody aftermath. Bodies lay where they had fallen, or been flung. The smashed remains of shelters fluttered in the last breath of the night wind. Blood oozed up through a thin crust of windblown sand. All was still, and then the shrill oscillating whine of a drivecoil split the silence. Ninos and his warrior force looked on, helpless, as the Daltrescan ship, bearing every living Quespodon on the planet, rose from Xhanchos and headed for the stars.

PART THREE:

To the Throne

I.

The Fugitive

Two full galactic years after his departure from Xhanchos, Kian Jorry found himself on the busy little trading world of Tricaps. His situation was not encouraging. He was alone, sole survivor of an unfortunate band; the last of the jewels was gone; the *Seraph* drifted in space with four dead men aboard. Worst of all, a pursuing force of Sternverein Security troopers were closing fast.

The blackjackets were persistent. Jorry had escaped them too often, and this time they were determined to take him. He was equally determined to elude them once more, but with no driveship and near-empty pockets, his prospects were bleak.

And yet Jorry was not downcast. The blackjackets might be close, but they had not yet arrived. He was alive and forewarned. There was still hope.

Jorry, nevertheless, took certain precautions. He let his hair grow long, warrior-style, and purchased a much-worn uniform from the First Rinn Expedition. No one on Tricaps knew his real name. Even a sharp-eyed Sternverein Security trooper would find it difficult to recognize him as a k'Turalp'Pa, much less as the fugitive Kian Jorry. He looked much like a Skorat now, and he swaggered through his role convincingly.

He was safe for the time being, but that was not enough. He needed someplace where he could be secure until the blackjackets gave up the search. But he wanted a comfortable haven; some barren rock in far isolation might offer safety, but at too high a price.

The time had come to make his plans and stick to

them. If he had not allowed himself to be swayed from his original plan to return directly to Boroq-Thaddoi, he would not be in trouble now. He would be wealthy. Of course, the others were worse off. Those who had shrunk from the prospect of a Q-world and urged a raid on a Sternverein merchant fleet instead, were all dead. Jorry lived, and while he lived he could think, and if he could think at all he could outsmart any pursuer.

And so he stayed quietly on Tricaps and thought out his situation. He could not help remembering the past, and a score of times he cursed Gariv's memory. But for that Skorat fool, Jorry would now be on some quiet world with Santrahaar, enjoying the present, forgetting the past, and looking forward to future triumphs. And now, thanks to Gariv, he was a ragged fugitive, alone, his funds almost gone.

Brooding on this one night, he took the pendant with the motion painting of Nikkolope from his tunic and studied it closely. A fine woman, this Queen of Thak. In a different way, she was as beautiful as Santrahaar. A Gafaal woman was a refuge and a paradise, a beauty to stun the senses and catch at the heart. But Nikkolope would be a partner, an ally against the galaxy. Santrahaar had been bred to conquer by surrendering; Nikkolope was born to rule at the side of an equal. She was the woman for a k'Turalp'Pa.

Deep in thought, Jorry went to the glass in his shabby room and studied his features closely. His dark, full beard was streaked with white, as Gariv's had been. Stripping off his tunic, he looked at the ragged white scar that he had carried since his first meeting with the blackjackets. Gariv had displayed a similar scar. Not identical, but similar. And Gariv was his height, though a bit heavier, and of similar coloring. It was conceivable, just barely conceivable, that if he could get to Gariv's homeworld of Skorat, Jorry might be able to pull off a successful impersonation.

He threw the tunic over his shoulders and sprawled on his pallet. This was an audacious plan. He thought on it, and laughed. It was ridiculous. First of all, without a driveship or enough to buy passage on one, he'd have to reach Skorat. And then he'd have to deceive Gariv's old friends and family. And his wife. Impossible. Suicidal.

But he was a k'Turalp'Pa. Nothing was too difficult for him, once he put his mind to it. Not Q-worlds, not black-jackets. And certainly not a planet full of dense, boastful Skorats.

And it was better to try this than to cower in a dirty little room on Tricaps and wait for his pursuers to burst in the door. It was simply a matter of planning. One thing at a time.

First, the ship.

The first necessary factor in Jorry's planning came into his grasp when the ancient driveship *Phoenix XXVII* landed on Tricaps. The ship was manned by two young starfarers who had found it drifting, an interstellar derelict with a crew of dust and dry bones, and had claimed it as their own. Its arrival on the planet caused a great sensation, for the *Phoenix XXVII* was no less than three galactic centuries old, a repository of items long since forgotten, hence of great potential value. The cargo of books alone—nine genuine Old Earth books, printed on paper—was worth the price of the ship.

The Tricapets were interested in the ship and its contents; Jorry cared more about the two starfarers. He learned that they had already begun negotiations for the sale of the *Phoenix XXVII* and the purchase of a fast little Third Stage scoutship with their profits. Jorry could learn nothing about the lean and taciturn elder crewman, but he found that the younger of the two, a Malellan named Whitby, was on his way to Gilead in search of information about his parents. Jorry was happy to hear this. It was his passage to Skorat.

He made his move the very next day, on the busy, crowded streets of Commerce City. It was no problem to spot the Malellan. He wore an old uniform from the *Phoenix XXVII*, and he literally sparkled as he moved through the scurrying throngs of little gray-clad Tricapets.

He was not much more than a boy, but he walked with confidence. His hair was plaited in the Skeggjatt style. His bright uniform, and the weapons he wore at his side, made him look like a figure from the ancient days.

Jorry kept him in sight at a safe distance and watched him stop in scoof parlors again and again—not, he was certain, because the youth enjoyed the scalding hot black beverage, but from sheer boredom. If one was not conducting business, there was little to do on this world.

At last, late in the day, when he was sure that his quarry would welcome the sight of another starfaring man, Jorry circled around him, raced through a building, and popped from the outway just as the Malellan approached. Jorry gaped for a moment, like a man who sees an impossible but welcome sight, and then rushed to the young man's side, jabbering away in the common tongue with the Tarquinian inflections the Mallelan used.

"By the stars, it's good to see another spaceman!" Jorry cried, wringing the youth's hand in welcome. "I've been in this bzzits' nest two months, surrounded by these poor, dull space-swindlers, and I'm slowly dying of boredom. Who are you, stranger, and where are you from, and where bound?"

The other looked him over before replying carefully, "My name's Del Whitby. I just came from the Skeggjatt system, bound for Gilead."

Jorry frowned in feigned perplexity, scratched his neck, and shook his grizzled head. "Gilead? I'm afraid that's one place I've never been. Where is it?"

"I'm hoping to find out," Del said.

Jorry weighed the remark for a moment, then burst into laughter. This was an unfamiliar sound on the streets of Commerce City, and passing Tricapets, after a nervous glance, gave the two a wide berth. "So you know where you're going, but you don't know where it is. I like your spirit, Del," he said earnestly, looking the young starfarer in the eye, dropping his gaze. "I was that way once myself, long ago. I wanted to see it all, go everywhere, experience everything . . . and I have. Believe me, I have."

After a moment's moody silence, he fixed Del with an intent look and asked, "Are you in a hurry, Del? Have you got time to buy an old spacebum a meal and listen to his stories?"

Del Whitby could not refuse. They found a place where the food was good and the noise of Tricapet jabbering and haggling was less strident than elsewhere, and after an enormous meal, over a fresh bottle of local wine—nothing at all like Stepmann green, but drinkable—Jorry told Del his history. It was, in many respects, the story of Kian Jorry, but it contained as well a substantial portion of the recent history of Gariv—particularly the bitter events that had kept him away from his kingdom and his beautiful queen for so long. He told of the Battle of the Three Systems and the smashing of the great Rinn fleet, and of his wandering in search of home. His knuckles whitened and his voice shook when he described his own capture by slavers when his ship was only a day away from Skorat. He told of Xhanchos and bondage to the pyramid builders, and here he became inventive. He had himself escaping alone from the Xhanchilion, crossing half a planet under the murderous desert sun, and being nursed back to health by the Gafaal princess Santrahaar.

Del was visibly moved by the account. Young as he was, he knew the pain and loneliness of long separation from loved ones. He himself had been carried off his homeworld by Daltrescan raiders, and was easily roused to sympathize with another's suffering. When Jorry had finished his sad tale, Del asked, "How far is Skorat from here?"

Jorry exulted inwardly, but his expression was one of profound gloom. "A long way, Del. It's out near Watson's Planet, where the great machine rules. A ship leaves here for Watson every few years, but the Tricapets are a hard-hearted lot. If I can't talk my way on as a crewman, they'll demand full passage, and I'll never be able to make it. I guess I'm at the end of a long, hard road."

His words had the desired effect. Del offered him a place on his new driveship. This was a good beginning, but only a beginning. He still had to get to Skorat. With this further objective in mind, he encouraged Del to talk about himself and as the youth explained his search, Jorry saw that he had come upon the resolution of all his difficulties.

Del was not born on Gilead. He was a foundling, sent to that peaceful and isolated world in a tiny escape craft from Pendelton's Base just before that outpost was destroyed. The only clue as to who had sent him was a cryptic notation on a scrap of paper.

Jorry asked to see the paper. He studied it, all the while searching his memory. In his long life of voyaging, he had heard many a tale of the Rinn Wars, and he knew of the destruction of Pendelton's Base and of a near-legendary Expedition Commander who had turned into an avenging demon upon the loss of his wife and infant son in the raid. The wife was a Malellan. Corey, the commander, was an Old Earther. The odds against their being Del's true parents were staggering, to be sure; but it was a plausible possibility, and that was all Jorry needed. Del was eager to hear news, and could be easily convinced. Once convinced, and thus indebted, he could be put to use at Jorry's convenience.

With a great show of reluctance, hesitating often, carefully qualifying every word, Jorry slowly let out the tale of Commander Corey and his lost family. Del listened avidly, hanging on every word. When Jorry was done, he asked, "You think this Corey might be my father?"

"It's possible," Jorry said cautiously. "Someone could have shoved an infant into an escape craft and gotten it off Pendelton before the Rinn struck. You've got Malellan features, Del, and you move like a Malellan, but you're much too big. You're built more like someone of the Old Earth bloodline, not a Malellan. Now, if your mother was Malellan and your father was Corey . . ."

After that, it was no problem to convince Del that only one course of action lay open to him: proceed to Watson's Planet, the information center of the galaxy, and learn all that could be learned about Commander Corey.

And the way to Watson took them near Skorat. Del could not refuse a stopover for the man who had furnished him this information.

Jorry had his transportation. The first phase of his plan was complete.

II.

The Decision

By the end of the long run to Skorat, Jorry had firmly settled on the main lines of his plan. It was a bold undertaking, but the more he thought on it, the better he liked it. To steal a kingdom was nothing new to him; but to steal at one stroke a kingdom, a queen, and another man's identity was a feat to be envied even by the k'Turalp'Pa.

He had carefully reviewed every scrap of information gleaned from Gariv during their acquaintance, and rooted the significant facts in his memory. After all this time, few would recall precise details of the past, and fewer still—not even the queen, Nikkolope—would be able to identify Gariv with absolute certainty. No one on Skorat could know that Gariv lay dead on Xhanchos, halfway across the galaxy. Their resemblance was close, and Jorry had carefully observed Gariv's mannerisms and gestures. He even had a convincing scar on his chest. He had no doubt that with boldness and assurance he could carry off the impersonation, reign in comfort until the Sternverein Security forces abandoned their search, and then, when he had had his fill of Gariv's life, his world, and his queen, move on. Meanwhile, he would put all the resources of Skorat to use in acquiring a new *Seraph* for his return to Boroq-Thaddoi. All things considered, his plan was excellent, and he was quite pleased with it and with himself.

As a precaution, he invited Del and his friend Grax to accompany him to the city of Thak. It seemed a sensible move. They carried weapons and were skilled in using them. Del was sympathetic, and Grax was restless for action, and both were convinced that they were bringing home a long-absent king. Should he be challenged, they might be useful.

Jorry guided them to a free landing in a spot Gariv had told of, and they set out for Thak on foot, at once. Inside the city gate they separated. They were to meet at the ship, the *Renegade*, at nightfall.

Jorry found Thak much as he had expected the chief city of a Skorat kingdom to be: old, badly kept, and dirty, with strong unpleasant odors much in evidence. The economy was based heavily on trettles, and the massive thick-horned beasts were everywhere in the cobbled streets. Nasty yellow insects trailed in clouds behind each beast, feeding indiscriminately on droppings or passers-by. Jorry decided that the returned monarch's first order would be for a general scrubdown of the streets, followed by a ban on animal traffic.

For some reason, many visitors were in Thak this day, and from the scraps of talk he overheard, Jorry learned that more were expected. A major celebration seemed to be at hand. To learn more, Jorry stopped at an inn, ordered some bread and cheese and a mug of the strong, sour-smelling beer, and sat down at the crowded public table, where commoners were served. He ate and drank in silence, listening to the conversation of three herdsmen. He was very careful to sit upwind of them. They went on about business matters for a time, but eventually one of them turned to the topic of the festivities.

"Good prices or bad," he said resignedly, "they're sold, every one, and I can enjoy myself without any worries."

"If you were smart, you'd worry about finding a place to sleep in safety. By nightfall, there won't be a room left in all of Thak," a second herdsman warned.

"I'll sleep outside the walls. It'll be safe now. All of Skorat observes peace at a time like this."

"Too bad it doesn't happen more often," said a third.

"Right you are. Last one I remember was over in Kabbrak, six herdings ago."

"Forigol's wedding?"

167

"That was it."

"Your memory's failing you, old-timer. Forigol's wedding was eight herdings back."

"Six, eight . . . what difference?" said the first speaker carelessly. "Royal weddings are few and far between, that's my point. The last one before Forigol was when Gariv married Nikkolope."

"She was no more than a girl. I remember it myself," the second herdsman said wistfully.

"Nikkolope's no longer a girl, I'll grant you that, but she's still the great beauty of Skorat. Sounitan's a lucky man."

"He is, he is. Any man on Skorat would gladly change places with him."

The third of the herdsmen said with a sigh, "Imagine . . . married to Nikkolope, ruling Thak with her at your side . . ."

Jorry showed no outward sign, but the words went through him like a blade of ice. To come this close, and have his prize snatched from him, would be maddening. He had to learn more; perhaps there was still a chance.

"Excuse me, friends, but I heard what you were saying and I can't keep my words back," he said, adopting a bluff, open manner, leaning forward over his bowl to look at each one in turn. "What troubles me is this—are we all sure that Gariv is dead?"

"You're not the only one to ask that, stranger," the first, oldest herdsman replied. "I'll say this: Queen Nikkolope is satisfied that he is. She's spoken to someone who witnessed his death on Xhanchos."

It took all his k'Turalp'Pa self-control to keep Jorry from throttling the information out of them; but true to his nature, he remained outwardly unmoved in the face of this impossible announcement. Something was badly amiss; either that, or someone else was plotting as boldly as he. There had been no witnesses to Gariv's death. And even if a legion of witnesses had stood in the throne room of Xhancholii, how would one of them have escaped to Skorat?

"Who was the witness?" Jorry asked.

"The bard . . . the skillman . . . ," said the youngest of the herdsmen, groping for the name.

"Alladale," his companion said in his aid. To Jorry, he added, "They say he's the true son of Alladale Anthemmaker, greatest of all the bards."

"That isn't so. Gariv bestowed the name for his deeds in battle," said the young herdsman.

Alladale . . . The name came back to Jorry, and he recalled Gariv's angry mention of the bard who had fled his court on Xhanchos. This was a complication, indeed.

"Where is the bard? Has he left Skorat?" Jorry asked.

"No, he's traveling among the royal cities. I haven't heard him myself—just missed him in Tavan—but I've spoken with some who have, and they say he's the best," the young herdsman said.

The second spoke up. "He'll be in Thak for the wedding. The lucky ones will hear him there."

"Lucky, indeed. To be one of the threescore . . ."

The older herdsman shook his head glumly. "Who knows where she'll go to do the choosing? If we could find that out, and be waiting when she arrives . . ."

Jorry listened to the details of the ancient custom by which the reigning partner in any Skorat royal marriage invited threescore subjects, chosen at random, to represent the people as guests at the wedding, at a place in the city undisclosed until the time of choosing. Jorry noted this fact, added it to what he had learned about Alladale, and left the inn to seek a place quiet and apart and consider the changed situation.

Alladale was a danger, no doubt of that. Perhaps the bard's presence in Thak was sufficient reason to abandon the entire plot. What, after all, was to be gained by persisting? Other worlds and other kingdoms abounded in the galaxy and a clever man could take what he wanted at less risk than the winning of the throne of Thak was likely to involve. Nikkolope, great beauty though she surely was, was not the only great beauty in the galaxy. Thak itself was hardly worth a lie, much less the risking of one's life: a grubby collection of stone, dirt, and timber on a backward planet populated by braggarts, brawlers, and some of the foulest-smelling herdsmen to be encountered anywhere. They would be a dreary lot to rule over, that was certain. This was decidedly a losing game, and to carry it further would be utter folly.

Jorry thought of all these things as he sat in a shaded alcove and looked out at the glittering harbor of Thak, where the broad, blunt-nosed trading boats with their colorful crescent sails rocked and bobbed on the gentle waves. It was a restful scene, a bright image of serenity and order that stood as a wordless advocate for the peaceful life. He felt the weight of a score of worlds in his bones, and the weariness of far travel in his blood. Time, the old enemy, was unconquered. It was catching up in its long race with Jorry. But Jorry knew he could win out yet. All he needed was a rest, and this harsh and ugly world offered the chance.

Jorry thought of a conversation by a fireside, long ago, when he had mocked the desire for rest and laughed at those who spoke of it. But now he felt the need. A peaceful life . . . The phrase came to mind, and with it came the memory of Santrahaar. She had spoken so often of the joyous prospect of their peaceful life together on some world far removed from Xhanchos and the barbarity of Gariv's rule. And to gratify his ignorant vanity, Gariv had killed her. It became clear to Jorry that his decision had been long made. He was going to reach for the throne of Thak. Gariv owed it to him. More important, he owed it to himself.

Four times had his plans been brought to nothing by the hand of another. First, he was swindled out of all he had by his own brother. Then the wealth of Boroq-Thaddoi had been lost through the bungling of his crew. Santrahaar had been taken from his arms by the impulsive violence of a fool. His last undertaking had been ruined by the meddling blackjackets who still pursued him. These defeats were enough; he had to go through with this plan. It was not for Nikkolope, or the throne, but for the sake of his own pride. Taking Gariv's throne and queen would give Jorry a threefold reward: a sanctuary from his pursuers, retribution on Gariv, and a base for his final expedition to Boroq-Thaddoi. He had no other course.

He would bring this off alone, unaided, with no one to betray him. That much he had learned. Others might be used, but never depended upon. They only disrupted the planning of wiser minds. The way to win was to play alone and depend on no one.

Once he had made his decision, Jorry turned his thoughts to the method. By late in the day, he had settled everything. It was really very simple. Since Alladale represented a threat, he had to be removed—and what better way to do it than by himself, in a face-to-face confrontation? Denounce the bard as a liar, accuse him of a plot, and strike him down on the spot before he could respond. It was exactly what Gariv would have done. If any objected, their objection would be proof of their part in Alladale's plot. So much for the bard.

Victory was still possible. He need only act with speed and decisiveness; a moment's hesitation and all was lost. But why should he hesitate? He was a k'Turalp'Pa among Skorats—a longeye among the blind, in the words of the old Onhla saying.

When the sun touched the horizon, Jorry rose to be about his business. One thing more was to be done: a palace official must be found who knew the place where Nikkolope would make the selection of guests the following day. A bribe to him, a bribe to the guards on duty at the site, and Jorry would have entry to the palace. It was all he required.

III.

The Choosing

Jorry was the last to return to the *Renegade,* well after
the long Skorat night had fallen. He told Del and Grax of
the day's developments and his plans for dealing with
them. The two starfarers received his news without enthu-
siasm. They were not fearful for themselves—two men
who board a derelict driveship and bring her across light-
centuries of empty space cannot be labeled timid—but
concerned for a companion's safety. They felt that he had
left too much up to chance.

"There's no alternative," Jorry responded to their objections. "Nikkolope makes the choice herself. That can't
be fixed."

Del shook his head unhappily. "Suppose Grax and I
don't get picked. You'll be in there alone."

"What if *you* don't get picked?" Grax demanded,
pointing at Jorry. "The wedding will come off, and you'll
be outside. Won't be able to do a thing."

"If that happens, I'll just have to think of a new plan,
Grax. But I think we'll be picked. We'll be waiting in the
right place, and I've bribed the guardsmen to see to it that
no one pushes ahead of us."

"Still, there's sure to be a crowd," Del said.

Jorry smiled and raised a hand. "I'm not finished, my
friend. I've also bribed Nikkolope's bearers to stop as
close to us as they can."

"Good move," Grax said approvingly.

"Think of it. Nikkolope will be set down near us. We'll
be among the first she sees—a man who's sure to arouse
her curiosity by his resemblance to her deceased hus-

172

band," Jorry said, tapping himself on the chest, and then, gesturing to the others, "and two otherworlders who can spread the word of her beauty, generosity, and magnificence on this day across the stars. Well?" He stopped, scratched his chest thoughtfully, and broke into a broad grin. "By the blazing rings, lads, I think I've squandered my last holdings on unnecessary bribes! It will be impossible for her *not* to choose the three of us!"

"I'm glad you're so confident. I have my doubts."

"I have great confidence, Del. Justice is on my side," Jorry said piously. "I've come to claim what's rightfully mine, and nothing will stop me."

"In case anyone tries, we'll do what we can," Grax promised.

Jorry volunteered to take the first watch. When the others turned in, they addressed their farewells to him as "Gariv." He found the name comfortable. By this time, he almost believed his own words. The throne of Thak *was* rightfully his—provided he could seize it. Justice *was* on his side—if one accepted the k'Turalp'Pa definition of justice.

Isolated as the *Renegade* was, Jorry saw no great need for caution. He spent his entire watch reviewing his plans for the next day. Once things were under way, he would have no time to deliberate. His choices would have to be automatic. If he once faltered, all was lost. By the time Grax relieved him, he was satisfied that all was ready. With no need for further consideration, he turned in and slept soundly until just before dawn.

By early morning, Jorry, Del, and Grax had joined the crowd at the Gate of the Nine Kings. According to Jorry's informant, this would be the place of choosing. From the look of things, and the air of excitement and expectancy all around him, Jorry judged it likely that others, too, were aware that this was to be the spot.

Soon after their arrival, a whisper spread through the crowd, growing almost at once to a roar: Nikkolope was on her way here, to this very gate. From streets and alleys and doorways, men and women poured into the already

173

crowded space before the gate. Jorry was separated from his companions, swept along by the milling, shouting mob that bore him forward. The queen's guardsmen had already begun to use their clubs to keep the crowd back. Jorry let himself be carried ahead, and when he was close to a guard he gave the prearranged signal. Without a sign of recognition, the guard drove back those on Jorry's left and right with sharp jabs of his long club and eased Jorry into a safe shelter between himself and the next guard. The outcries around him increased, some of them turning to yelps of pain, a few of them outraged curses. But so loud that they drowned out all else were the shouts of love and praise for Nikkolope and her chosen consort.

The pair came in view, reclining side by side on heaped cushions in a carriage drawn by a dozen liveried servants, and Jorry had his first glimpse of the woman he meant to claim. Nikkolope was more beautiful than he had imagined, a matured and fulfilled version of the fresh young bride in Gariv's motion painting. She was statuesque and slender of figure. Her robing was bright and rich in texture. On her head was a jeweled crown, and jeweled bracelets clattered and rang with every wave of her hands. The color and opulence of these trappings gave her the air of a barbaric empress, but her expression was one of poise and sophistication. Jorry found her fascinating, and he had to tear his eyes away to study his rival.

Prince Sounitan was a muscular lad, younger than the queen and clean-featured. The people called him handsome and found his surly, self-satisfied expression attractive, but Jorry considered him a pompous oaf—no different, indeed, from most Skorat males young and old of the warrior class. He hated him at a glance. Sounitan flexed a sinewy forearm, admiring the play of muscles; he gazed languidly out at the mob, and clearly gloried in the show of homage and fealty. Jorry frowned. This smug boy had no place by the side of a woman like Nikkolope. It would be a service to remove him.

Jorry returned his attention to the Queen of Thak. The royal carriage had halted almost directly before him, and

174

she was announcing her intention to choose the representatives of the common people from the crowd here gathered. A great burst of cheering followed her words, and continued as she stepped gracefully from the carriage and formed her guard around her. She moved forward, her eyes sweeping across the multitudes. Her gaze met Jorry's and rested on him for an instant before passing on. She gave no sign of recognition, but he had seen the question flicker in her eyes and perceived her momentary hesitation. He felt a surge of genuine admiration for the woman. Her poise, her self-possession, were magnificent. No other woman, nor any man, could have absorbed such a shock unwavering.

He watched her come closer. She paused to question an eager citizen, and in the middle of his speech turned from him leaving him open-mouthed. She next exchanged pleasantries with a young couple, laughed gently and affectionately at the girl's words, and made a sign that they had been chosen. The crowd exploded into a new outburst of cheers, and Nikkolope moved on, slowly, smiling as she proceeded, drawing out a ritual she seemed to find pleasurable. At last she stood before Jorry, and looked at him in silence before asking his name. Politely and respectfully, he gave her a false one.

"Not a Skorat name, and yet you look to be one of us. Are you from Thak?" she asked.

"I am, Your Majesty, but I've been a long time away. I've only recently come home."

Her eyes remained fixed on his, and the look in them was a challenge. "It's a bad thing to be away too long. Have you a wife? Did she wait for you?"

"My wife is considered by some to be the equal of the Queen of Thak in beauty. And I believe she's waited, although . . ."

"Go on," Nikkolope commanded.

"Well, Your Majesty, in my absence, a vain and foolish boy has paid court to her. I place no blame on her for this, but I mean to punish the youngster. Honor demands it."

"Have you spoken to her of this?"

"Not yet, Your Majesty. But I shall before this day is out."

She studied him closely, and he met her eyes without flinching. At last she turned to a guard and said, "Such trust deserves a reward. I choose him." Without another glance, she moved on.

He fell into place behind the guard, joining the young couple selected before him. The first, and most dangerous, hurdle was past. The crowd gave another cheer as he took the medallion of the queen's favor and placed it around his neck, but he scarcely heard them.

He did not see the two young starfarers, nor did he care to. His hope was that they had not been chosen. Now, at last, he was truly on his own. No cowardly crew of bunglers and traitors could thwart his plans this time. On all of Skorat, no one but Nikkolope could stop him now, and she seemed uncertain of his true identity. Their exchange before the crowd had been too subtle for these Skorat clods to follow, but each of them understood the other clearly. The resolution was soon to come.

IV.

The Homecoming

Tradition and custom and innumerable ceremonies hallowed by time constituted a strong and binding force on the world of Skorat, and none were more scrupulous in observation of the ancient usages than the ruling families of Thak. For them, it was ignominous simply to be born, to come of age, to do battle, marry, grow old, and die without public rites to mark every noteworthy date. Farmers, herdsmen, and otherworlders might be satisfied to make a silent passage from life to death, but not a warrior noble. For a member of that class, every step of the progress from infancy to final rest was accompanied by its own elaborate and inflexible ritual, and the higher one's rank and greater the occasion, the more grandiose the observance became.

A royal marriage was a rare event of great significance, and the attendant ceremonies occupied a period of time equivalent to more than a galactic month. On a warlike world such as Skorat, where nineteen royal cities and hundreds of smaller principalities lived in a state of constant hostility, such public merrymaking would be impossible were it not for the first and most rigid of all Skorat traditions: A royal wedding, a coronation, and the visit of a bard invoked an automatic truce. To violate such a time meant death.

A rich body of Skorat legend dealt with the conflicts arising from this law. A guest might make any accusation, level the vilest slander against his company or his host, and rest secure from violence as long as the festivities endured. No weapon could be raised against him. His host was bound by honor to protect him. Understandably, the aftermath of any public ceremony on Skorat was an outbreak of general warfare, but the festivities themselves remained peaceful.

For this, the first of the celebrations of the wedding of Queen Nikkolope and the consort Prince Sounitan, the great central hall of the palace had been turned into a refectory. Near one end of the columned chamber two thrones were set on a raised dais. Nikkolope was seated on the higher throne, with Sounitan at her right hand. Behind them, closing off the farther end of the hall, rose a screen of carved and painted wood, through which the servants entered and left.

Though they were much given to ritual, the Skorats were not as a people fond of either speeches or delay. To Jorry's surprise, once the chosen guests had entered the palace, the feasting began almost immediately. The nobles were shown to their places along the outer walls, while the common guests were left to seat themselves in the center. Jorry had scarcely settled at the middle table, close to the thrones and directly facing Sounitan, than one server poured his wine and a second placed a dish of smoking tidbits before him. Without a toast or a greeting or a word of thanks to their hosts, the diners fell to. Glancing up, Jorry saw that Sounitan had already emptied his goblet and Nikkolope had sampled the first dish.

Jorry drank little, but ate as heartily as the others. He pounded the table top and the arms of his chair to show approval, Skorat style, of the musicians' performance; he wept or cheered at the songs and stories, praised the grace and vigor of the dancers, and all the while kept his eyes on Nikkolope, waiting for her expression to signal the right moment. Their eyes met often, but never did she betray her feelings, and Jorry's admiration for her grew.

In the end it was not the queen but her bard who moved Jorry to action, and he did it unawares. Jorry had noticed the man in Nikkolope's gaudy livery circulating among the nobles; he had judged him a minor courtier and dismissed him from his attention. But when the man

178

at his left nudged him and said, "There's Alladale, the queen's bard. Greatest in the galaxy, they say. Do you think he'll sing for us?" Jorry tensed.

This was the Alladale who had told the queen of Gariv's death. Whether he spoke from knowledge or was simply saying the words he knew she expected—perhaps wished—to hear, this bard was a danger. If he had seen Gariv, he would be sure to note Jorry's resemblance to him; if he had not, then he was carrying out some plot of his own, and was no less a threat. The only thing to do in this tangle of conspiracies was to move first, dispose of Sounitan, then Alladale, and proclaim himself the returned king of Skorat. The time to act was at hand.

"Let there be silence!" Jorry cried in a loud voice, rising in his place. "I have news of great interest for our beloved queen!"

All talk at his table stopped at once. Attentive silence spread out around him, as noiseless rings radiate from a stone dropped in still water. Loud laughter from a group of nobles at a far table died abruptly. He saw guards moving toward him and looked to Nikkolope. She gestured, and the guards halted in place.

"You are free to speak, stranger. Tell us your news," she commanded.

Her voice was firm but calm. It carried to every corner of the chamber. Jorry licked his lips, took a deep breath, and plunged ahead, staking everything on one bold bluff. "The true king of Skorat lives!" he roared, raising his arms high in the monarchic salute. "Gariv has returned from the dead to claim his throne, his kingdom, and his queen!"

A great babble of voices rose all around him, but he stood firm, his eyes fixed on Nikkolope, who sat as cool and self-possessed as the young girl in the motion painting. It burst upon Jorry that she was not deceived and never had been. She did not for a moment believe that he was Gariv, but it made no difference to her. If he could oust Sounitan she would accept him; if not, he deserved whatever death he suffered. Nikkolope was let-

179

ting the interloper play his hand and calmly observing the result. She would back no one until he was the victor.

What a woman for a k'Turalp'Pa! Jorry thought exuberantly—there'd be no match for us in the galaxy!

When the uproar caused by his words had subsided, Nikkolope asked, "If Gariv has returned, let him speak for himself. Where is he?" Her tone was challenging, as it had been earlier, when they had bandied words at the time of choosing. She sees it all! She *knows,* Jorry thought, and vowed to win her.

"Here! I am Gariv!" he cried in a mighty voice.

Sounitan sprang to his feet and pointed accusingly at him. "You lie! Impostor!"

"Usurper!" Jorry countered, shaking his fist at the prince.

Sounitan sank back on his throne, smiling. "Guards, take this beggar to the gates and impale him," he ordered. At the command, two guards armed with javelins closed on Jorry. The crowd gasped at this break of the ancient code. Nikkolope looked on, content to let the rivals play out their match unimpeded.

Jorry could have dispatched the two easily with his knives. But Gariv would not have done so, and now he was Gariv. Instead, he snatched a heavy pitcher from the table. Sidestepping the first guard's lunge, he brought the pitcher around in a backhanded swing that caught him full on the temple. The blow, added to his own momentum, sent the stunned guard reeling against the other. Jorry seized the fallen javelin, drove the butt end into the second guard's belly, then jumped over his doubled-up body and took a stance atop the table. It was time for the final move that would decide everything.

"Death to the usurper! Gariv has returned!" he cried, and launched the javelin at Sounitan with all his strength behind it.

It was over in seconds. Even as the javelin left Jorry's hand, Sounitan uncoiled like a cat, with a speed and grace that belied his languid manner. In a single flowing motion he plucked the missile from the air, reversed it, cocked back his arm, and sent the javelin straight at his assailant.

Jorry felt the hard blow on his chest, the sudden rush of pain as the point tore into him, forcing its way through the ribs and bursting out his back. He clutched at the shaft, his eyes wide, and opened his mouth to speak. No words came. He knew it was all over, everything was over, he was going to die and all his plans were ruined, no one to blame, all his own doing, his mistakes, his fault. No clumsy Thanist had undone him this time; no foolish vain king had snatched the prize from him; he had tried his best and lost, lost everything, lost forever.

The room swam before his eyes. He saw Nikkolope's impassive face, Sounitan beside her, triumphant. He felt himself falling backward, and then he felt no more.

The unpleasant incident was over. Nikkolope spoke briefly to reassure her guests, the talk resumed, the musicians played a merry song, and the feast went on. Jorry's body was removed, dragged beyond the gate, and thrown on a refuse heap. The guests ate and drank their fill, and late at night the last of them made his unsteady way from the palace.

For Nikkolope and her guards, the day did not end with the feast. She retired to her private apartment and summoned the commander of the palace guard. Before he arrived, Sounitan came to her. It was their first time alone since the feast, and she received him coldly.

"The people will have much to talk of," Sounitan greeted her, striking a regal pose. "It will be long before anyone challenges the majesty of Thak again."

"If you could think as well as you can throw a javelin, Sounitan, you'd be a formidable king."

"What do you mean?"

"I mean that you are a buffoon," Nikkolope said patiently. "True, you are a handsome buffoon, strong, and I have no doubt that you adore me, but your stupidity makes you dangerous." He gaped at her, sputtered an attempt at speech, but she silenced him and went on, "Today you violated host law in the palace of Thak. Did it not occur to you, when you demonstrated your prowess for your loving followers, that Skorat nobles were present?" At his crestfallen silence, she added contemptuously, "I see it did not. And now can you tell me how we are to convince them of their safety here during the remaining ceremonies? They have seen you slay one guest. They might wonder which of them will be next."

"What was I to do? He attacked. I only returned the weapon he threw."

"You set the guards on him, Sounitan. That might be construed as an attack, to which he reacted as any man would."

"He accused me . . . claimed to be Gariv himself!"

"I heard his words," Nikkolope said with some irritation.

Sounitan, who had grown more frustrated with each exchange, finally blurted, "But we know Gariv is dead! This man was an impostor—he may have been sent to delay our marriage in hopes of weakening your rule!"

Nikkolope looked at him for a moment before replying and then said in a voice that chilled him, "My marriage has no effect on my rule. Understand that, Sounitan, and cherish no illusions."

Chastened, he said, "I meant only . . . perhaps he hoped to create confusion . . . unrest among the people."

"It is possible. And all the more reason to take him alive, and not kill without thinking. Besides, we have only the word of the bard that Gariv is dead."

"Would he dare to lie?"

Nikkolope yawned. "Perhaps. All men lie."

The arrival of the guard captain ended their talk. The queen turned to him, an expression of anticipation on her fine features. "What of Alladale?" she demanded at once.

"He's nowhere to be found, Your Majesties," the captain reported, glancing from Nikkolope to her consort, and back to the queen.

"*Majesties?!*" Nikkolope shrilled in a burst of rage, rising and striking the captain a staggering blow with her ringed hand. "Majesties, indeed! Know, guardsman—and

182

you, too, prince—that Thak has one ruler, and I am she. I share my rule with no one."

"Yes, Your Majesty. Yes, of course," the captain said, trembling before her anger, afraid even to raise a hand to wipe the blood from his cheek. "I spoke without thinking, Majesty. Forgive me, please."

Nikkolope seated herself, glared at him, and at last said, *"You* are forgiven. The next man who speaks so without thinking will regret it deeply. Now, to business— what trace of the bard Alladale?"

"None, Your Majesty. He's disappeared completely."

"He was in league with the impostor. I suspected him all along, from the day he turned up here calling himself by a dead man's name," Sounitan growled.

"You suspected nothing," Nikkolope said matter-of-factly. "You disliked the bard because I showed him favor. I doubt his complicity."

Sounitan frowned and looked dubious. "Can you believe in such coincidence?"

"I believe nothing yet. I want the bard. We will hear his own story, all of it." To the guard captain she said simply, "Find him." When he had departed, she dismissed Sounitan. He protested, but left when she repeated the order sharply and turned from him to look out the narrow window. To his farewell, she responded, "I will summon you."

Nikkolope was troubled, and the realization that by her actions she was revealing her inner turmoil only troubled her the more. The intruder's appearance at such a time had been a cruel prank of fate, and its possible significance, as well as its repercussions, worried her. Like all Skorats, she believed in omens, but she was sufficiently wise and experienced to know that an omen can be interpreted in many ways. The name of Gariv had been raised at her remarriage, after his presumed death. Why? Could the interloper have been Gariv? After all this time. . . . He looked much like Gariv, that was true, and even his manner. . . . But all these things would be copied by a clever impostor. Even so, he might have been a better consort than Sounitan. Impostor or not, he had courage, and he had planned well. Sounitan's agility could not have been foreseen; until this day, she herself had not suspected it.

She reflected for a time on the possibility of other, more dangerous talents still lying hidden and unsuspected in the prince. He was not a man to impress one as a plotter, that was certain . . . but that might be all the more cause to fear him. What he had done today could be forgiven—he had not cast the javelin, merely returned it on his attacker—but it might also be judged a breach of host law. That would mean the end of Sounitan. It might be necessary.

She sighed and turned from the window. The prince was a fool, perhaps a dangerous fool, but she was fond of him. Gariv had been much like that long ago, when he fought for the right to wed her.

The soft knock at the chamber door startled her, even though she had been awaiting it. When the guard opened it cautiously, she did not wait for him to speak, but signaled the caller inside.

A tall, slender, white-haired man entered. He moved across the room in haste, limping slightly, and threw himself down on a couch with easy familiarity, stretching out his long legs. He let the concealing cloak fall away. His lined face was handsome in the same way as Nikkolope's gentler features. The visitor sighed wearily, clutched her hand in greeting, and shook his head.

"Well? Does he have the scar?" she demanded.

"He has a scar. But that proves nothing."

"Nothing? The scar on his chest and my painting around his neck prove nothing?"

The man raised a hand and let it fall. "A scar can be duplicated, my dear. And so can a motion painting. Remember, this impostor was playing for a queen and a throne. . . ."

"Still you say 'impostor.' Even after you've seen the scar on his chest," she said thoughtfully.

"I knew Gariv well for five herdings before you set

eyes on him. I would recognize him, and I say that the man who died today was not Gariv."

She turned to him, her face drawn with uncertainty. "After so long, father, how can you be certain? Even *I* could not be sure."

"He undid himself, my dear," the man said gently. "I spoke to the guards who dragged him out. They heard his last words—"

"Tell me!"

"They say he called himself a trickster. He spoke the word twice. Isn't that proof he was a fraud?"

She reflected on this news for a time, pacing the length of her chamber and returning at last to where her father sat. "Trickster . . . isn't that what Quespodons call their Over-being? He might have been. . . ."

Her father looked at her sharply, and spoke with an edge of disdain in his voice. "He was not a Quespodon, and that much is obvious. He was a Skorat, or some breed close to ours. No one mistakes a Quespodon for a Skorat, my dear."

Nikkolope settled beside him and rested her head on his shoulder. "He was one of us. I know that, father," she said.

"Well, then. Would Gariv die mumbling of a Quespodon god?"

She straightened, nodded her head, and rose. "He would not, of course," she said firmly. "I thank you, father. You've reassured me."

He rose and embraced her, then he left, limping slightly but moving with practiced speed and silence from the chamber. Nikkolope, left alone, thought on the day's events. The impostor had caused much turmoil in Thak by his brief appearance.

And he was an impostor, she told herself once again. The scar meant nothing. His words before the gate meant nothing. He was an impostor. She had to believe that.

But one thing still troubled her. When the impostor declared himself at the feast, he spoke of reclaiming his throne, his kingdom, and his queen. Gariv would have

185

spoken so. An impostor, in the queen's presence, would have put the queen first, not last. She was sure of that. Only Gariv. . . . But he was dead, and it was pointless to think of him.

She looked out the window, seeking a sign. Overhead, the stars wheeled onward through their cold configurations, unaware, unfeeling, isolated. No sign was given.

The Seraph II

Planetfall loomed on the screens of the *Seraph II*. From his post on the bridge, Axxal observed the planetary disc floating pale and silent before him and felt a momentary anxiety at the thought of what might lie ahead. But he mastered his qualms, issued the necessary orders, and prepared for landing. He and his crew had already overcome many obstacles. This was one more.

His people were a hard lot to lead, and the long close confinement of drivespeed travel made them no more tractable. Vaxxt did his best to keep the burden from Axxal's shoulders, but the Quespodons saw only Axxal as their leader. A surrogate was not respected.

What Axxal found almost maddening was the frequency with which, having begged for his judgment, they rejected it to follow some foolish notion of their own, to the harm of all involved. He was learning, painfully, the frustrations of leadership.

Oft-repeated arguments and exhortations echoed in his memory. He had wrangled bitterly with the Quespodons from the very start of this voyage. Scarcely were they aloft when he had had to dissuade them from a near-unanimous decision to return to the homeworld. That was his first and most difficult victory. Then had come the inevitable demand that they set down for a time on a world where they might enjoy the companionship of women after the long abstinence of space. Again he denied their wish. His command was clearcut: A Quespodon would marry only a Quespodon, and never one from the homeworld. They shouted, and threatened, and

187

denounced him as a worse tyrant than the Xhanchilion—but they obeyed his edict. They grumbled, but they obeyed. He had won.

Again and again he exhorted them, instilling his message of pride. He spoke to them at every opportunity—singly, in small groups, in large clusters, and always his final words were the same: We were the first. We were the best. Never forget.

He felt himself winning their faith as he had won their obedience. They began to trust him and believe him. A time arrived when no more objections greeted his message. They now listened to his words and accepted them. And even then, when he had their trust, Axxal held back their ultimate destination.

He had planned methodically since those anxious days on Xhanchos. They landed first on Wyttyp, where a small band of Quespodons were known to have settled three centuries earlier. When they lifted off, every Quespodon on that isolated world had joined them. Twice more they touched down for necessary supplies. Now the time for the final planetfall was at hand.

The voice of a crewman roused Axxal from his reverie. The time for manual landing procedure was near. He acknowledged the report and moved to the helm.

Three watches out, Axxal had assembled everyone aboard and announced their destination. Quespodons were a credulous breed. They might mistrust their chosen leaders, but they placed blind faith in every rumor, legend, and whispered tale. Their reaction was as Axxal had anticipated.

"You can't land there, Captain! We'll dissolve! We'll nova!" they cried, horrified. Or else they gaped and said, "There are monstrous things stalking those worlds—we'll be eaten alive!" or, "The whole sector is full of Rinn with weapons more powerful than anything we know!"

But Axxal knew otherwise. Building slowly and patiently on their grudging trust, he made them accept what he had come to believe and the plan he had made.

By Axxal's side hung a long blade with a twisted

188

handle, a memento of the skeletons falling to dust in the corridors under Boroq-Thaddoi. In his tunic he carried a precious stone taken from one who had fallen victim to the flapping thing that had killed Bral. He had held that stone back from Jorry, but not out of greed. He had wanted tangible proof of the things he had seen.

Whatever treasure lay below the citadel, its guardians were dead now, crushed under a mountain of stone. But Quespodons had the strength to move that rubble aside as if it were a mound of pebbles, and all the time they needed to accomplish the task. If it were to take generations, they could spare them. Time was their greatest resource. If at last the task proved impossible, or fruitless, there was still the great door of jewels. Axxal remembered the way. He knew the path over the mountains, the mouth of the underground river; he remembered the entry that stood open awaiting them, and he knew the turns and byways of the passages within.

He felt no fear, for now he knew that no nameless horrors lurked on Boroq-Thaddoi. The enemies were living creatures. He had faced them once and escaped to return stronger, forearmed. Under his guidance, the Quespodons would overcome.

But the talk of Leddendorf's treasure was, he knew, for the others. That was something they could grasp, and dream on. The thought of tangible wealth would give them courage for the undertaking. A different lure had drawn Axxal back to the quarantined world and its dangers. Leddendorf's wealth would smooth the path of a reborn people, to be sure; but there were far more valuable treasures buried on Boroq-Thaddoi.

Axxal recalled something Jorry had said on the plain before the citadel, as their band looked on the empty driveships of those who had come before: "Think of it, Axxal . . . there may be hundreds of ships on this world." Since leaving Xhanchos, Axxal had thought of little else. Ships . . . a fleet of them in which to seek out others of their kind and create a new race of Quespodons on nurturing planets far from their blighted homeworld.

Beneath all the hopes, all the aspirations, all the plans for his people, one suspicion stirred deep in Axxal's mind. It frightened him. It was too big a thought to deal with now; he was not ready. Perhaps later, when his mind was accustomed to thinking and reasoning and envisioning fantastic possibilities, he would be able to handle such ideas. Now, it only confused and disturbed him. It might better be left to the clearer minds of his children, and their children. And yet it persisted.

Again and again he remembered those enigmatic skeletons. What had those voyagers been seeking, ages before Leddendorf's treasure lay in the vaults? Only another, more ancient, treasure? Or had they set out in search of lost knowledge and been undone at last by greed? The citadel itself was virtually unexplored—who could tell what wonders it held? Something had drawn travelers to Boroq-Thaddoi from other worlds, perhaps even from other galaxies. What could it be?

Axxal had listened to Quespodons from the homeworld tell in halting phrases of the ruins that stood in the wastes of Dumabb-Paraxx, titanic shapes from an age beyond memory. They were said to be the work of starfarers from remote antiquity. Making every allowance for the exaggerations of homesickness and the childish boasting of the narrators, Axxal still found in the stories testimony to things beyond the capacity of any living race. They drew his mind to the citadel on Boroq-Thaddoi. It, too, had outlasted the memory of its builders. It might be that the same race had built both.

Axxal knew the tales of the race that had crossed the galaxy when the worlds were young and empty, and been—in legend, if not in fact—lifebringers and builders until they disappeared into mystery. If the same race had built the ruins on his homeworld and on Boroq-Thaddoi, then it was possible—however remotely, it was possible—that the First Travelers were Quespodons. Not the creatures of the present, slow of mind, disfigured of body, underlings to the galaxy, but a breed of unfallen giants from the ages before some homeworld cataclysm had turned them into stunted half-men.

Panel lights flashed before Axxal's eyes, commanding his attention. This was the hardest part of the voyage for him. One miscalculation could bring the *Seraph II* toppling to the surface and ground her forever. He reached for the controls. At the familiar sound of Vaxxt's crutch on the metal deck, he turned and nodded to his second-in-command.

"Almost there," Vaxxt said expectantly.

"Yes. How is morale?"

"No one's afraid any more. You've convinced them that we can handle anything on this world."

"We can," Axxal said.

"How about you?" Vaxxt lowered his voice and added, "A manual landing is hard. Most starfarers avoid them."

Axxal laid his stubby hands on the control plates and turned to his friend. "I can do it, Vaxxt," he said. "I learned from a master."

The *Seraph II* came gently down on the barren uplands of Boroq-Thaddoi. A hard day's march would bring them to a green valley, and fresh water, a sheltered haven from the wind and cold. A race could live here unmolested by greedy otherworlders who sought only to exploit their strength. A race could grow, and relearn its past, probe the citadel for its secrets and revive knowledge buried and lost for ages.

In twelve generations of slow recovery, Axxal's people had come far. Given twenty, fifty, a hundred generations to grow and recover, the Quespodons would be a race of beings to triumph over time and space. The challenge of a quarantined world was ahead of them. But they would face that challenge, and they would overcome. There were other, greater challenges ahead.

Axxal had begun something. He knew that he would not live to see the end of his work, but he could dream of it. When the Quespodons were ready, the galaxy awaited. And beyond lay all the universe.

ALL TIME BESTSELLERS
FROM POPULAR LIBRARY

☐ THE BERLIN CONNECTION—Simmel	08607-6	1.95
☐ THE BEST PEOPLE—Van Slyke	08456-1	1.75
☐ A BRIDGE TOO FAR—Ryan	08373-5	2.50
☐ THE CAESAR CODE—Simmel	08413-8	1.95
☐ DO BLACK PATENT LEATHER SHOES REALLY REFLECT UP?—Powers	08490-1	1.75
☐ ELIZABETH—Hamilton	04013-0	1.75
☐ THE FURY—Farris	08620-3	2.25
☐ THE HAB THEORY—Eckerty	08597-5	2.50
☐ HARDACRE—Skelton	04026-2	2.25
☐ THE HEART LISTENS—Van Slyke	08520-7	1.95
☐ TO KILL A MOCKINGBIRD—Lee	08376-X	1.50
☐ THE LAST BATTLE—Ryan	08381-6	2.25
☐ THE LAST CATHOLIC IN AMERICA—Powers	08528-2	1.50
☐ THE LONGEST DAY—Ryan	08380-8	1.95
☐ LOVE'S WILD DESIRE—Blake	08616-5	1.95
☐ THE MIXED BLESSING—Van Slyke	08491-X	1.95
☐ MORWENNA—Goring	08604-1	1.95
☐ THE RICH AND THE RIGHTEOUS —Van Slyke	08585-1	1.95

Buy them at your local bookstores or use this handy coupon for ordering: